"The Dreamer"
by Luis Aira
Cover Art by Edward WaltonWilcox
Luis Aira Copyright © 2010
Registered ® WGA
ISBN# 978-0-578-05347-9

ALSO BY LUIS AIRA

Somewhere

THE DREAMER

Luis Aira

Luis Aira

Dream well.

I
The Bottle Under the Tree

Something fell through the branches and hit the ground with a thump. The leaves swung back into place like closing curtains sending a multitude of apples rolling into the hollow. Old Slim lifted his head. It was dawn and the tree was glowing.

"Can't taste the cherry brandy," he thought. "This is odd. Where did the night go?"

That is when he noticed a young stranger who sat next to him leaning against the tree trunk with eyes closed. He studied the face; so beautiful, so full of life, so familiar.

"Pssst, you there," the old timer whispered. "Are you sleeping?" But the young stranger was not listening; he was immersed in his own thoughts.

Something. What? He had to remember. The young man just couldn't put his finger on it. That's as far as his memory would go. He opened his eyes and looked at the world. Resting against a tree on top a knoll, he had a thought. Perhaps he had always been here. Perhaps the knoll and the tree had appeared around him. The breeze brushed his face, perfumed with the sweet scent of apples. He looked at the branches above him and stared at the ripening fruits. Sky, knoll, tree, apple. Life. Words appeared in his mind. Where was he? Why couldn't he remember—and why didn't he care to? Perhaps he had something to forget; or perhaps nothing had happened yet. He had no idea who he was or even what he looked like, but he was enjoying the moment immensely. Breathing the scent of apples under the tree. Delightful.

"I'm Slim. What's your name?" he heard a voice say. An old man wearing a shabby suit and fedora lay in the grass on the other side of the tree.

"I don't know," he said without thinking.

"How long've you been there?"

"I just opened my eyes ... What are we?" he asked, touching the thick solid trunk. "What is this?"

"You're a human being and this here's a tree. I don't recall you last night drinking with me."

"I am a human being."

"Sure looks like it."

"Tell me, what do I look like?"

"What?"

"Do I look like you?"

"Hell no! I'm an old man and you're only a cub. You're crazier than I thought, boy. Where did you come from?"

"What do I look like?" the young man insisted. "Please describe me."

"Well ... you're young. Must be early twenties. You look a baby to me. Brown hair, brown eyes ... need a shave."

"So I'm young?"

"I've seen wine older than you."

The old man crawled around the base of the tree and sat next to the curious questioner.

"You've got a screw loose, kid," he said with a fatherly smile, "but you're a good person, I can tell."

"Slim," the young man whispered, "what are we doing here?"

"Like it? It's a real nice spot."

"It's lovely ..." He took a deep breath. The sweet air filled his lungs. Overwhelmed by a sense of well-being, he turned to Slim, puzzled.

"How did I get here?"

"How should I know? I was sleeping. I heard something fall through the leaves. How did you find this place?"

"I don't know … but this is where I am."

"You can't remember?"

"I can only remember being here next to you … that's all."

"Well I hope I'm not squatting with a ghost," old Slim replied. He kissed the rabbit's foot that hung from his neck and made the sign of the cross.

"A ghost? What is that?"

"Don't they have Halloween where you're from? A ghost is the spirit of someone who's dead."

The young man listened in awe. Several moments passed. "Are you a ghost?" he finally asked.

Slim was spooked. Maybe that bottle of brandy had got him at last and he was dead; how else to explain the sweet scent of apple blossoms out of season and this wonderful sense of peace? And what of the young stranger showing up from nowhere? Is he an angel—or the Angel of Death? What is he smiling at?

"Oh—I'm alive!" Slim exclaimed. He stared at the empty bottle on the grass nearby and retraced his steps. He had been dropped off at a truck stop the night before; from there he walked to a liquor store and got a pint of "pain killer," as he called the cheap cherry brandy. After that he headed toward his secret spot to get a good night's sleep. It was far from the highway and safe, a beautiful place beyond an orchard where the farmer never checked and an old apple tree had grown wild beyond its cousins.

Slim recalled no accidents or apparitions before or after; he got to the apple tree soon after sunset, and the sweetness of the brandy took over. The last thing he remembered was climbing to the treetop and hiding the bottle in his secret hole among the branches, high and away from the reach of scoundrels. He had awoken ten minutes ago with the bottle on the ground and the stranger asleep on the other side of the tree. Slim was mighty perplexed.

"I don't remember meeting anyone else," the young man said, breaking the silence. "You are the only person I know."

"What about the people before me?" Slim asked. The stranger didn't answer; he leaned against the tree and enjoyed the morning sun on his face. Old Slim sighed, reminding himself that a ghost wouldn't sunbathe or ask so many questions. Yet something was different about this boy. Slim was reluctant to find out what it was.

"Hey kid," the old man said.

"Yes?"

"Am I dreaming?"

"I don't know, are you?"

"Don't think so," Slim replied, giving his own arm a pinch.

"What is dreaming?" the young man asked.

Slim remained quiet, intrigued that his head didn't hurt in spite of the nightly cheap liquor. He studied his companion and came to a conclusion. The kid was just a lost soul, strange, but homeless nevertheless, so he decided to take him under his wing and show him the tricks of the trade.

"You need to meet more people," the elder began, concerned for his new young friend.

"Why?"

"Boy, it ain't my business, but here you are in the middle of a field with the only person you know, and … well … it just ain't right for a good young man."

"Oh. So what should I do?"

"Make something of yourself!"

"What am I now?"

Slim considered the question; the kid seemed so happy, untouched and pure; he could not recall ever before meeting someone like him.

"I don't know," he answered, "but you've got to grow like this tree! Look at them apples." He pointed to the hanging fruits. "Do you understand? You still have not told me your name."

"Well … I'm not too sure. I think I'd like that name. It feels good."

"What name?"

"How about Apple?"

"You can call yourself whatever you want, son. Names change all the time. I used to be George Harriet Remington the Third, but now I go by Slim. Nice to make your acquaintance," the old man said, tipping his fedora. "Got any liquor? Mine must've fallen out of the tree while I was under it, snoozin'."

"Apple it is!" cried the young fellow, "I like it very much! But what is liquor?" he asked, confused.

"Never you mind," Slim responded. "I was only foolin'. I see you're not a drinker."

The stranger looked happy, and Slim—who could not for the life of him recall a happy moment—considered that maybe the curious stranger knew something he did not. He stopped asking questions and giving advice and decided instead to share the dawn, sitting quietly next to Apple.

"Does this place have a name?" Apple asked, after several minutes.

"Eden Orchards," Slim replied. "This here ain't really heaven; there are people out there!" He chuckled to himself.

"Tell me more," Apple pressed, admiring the sky. "Where is this place?"

"This is my secret hiding place. Don't go tellin' folks about it. They'll be parking on the grass before you know it. Boy, you should try to remember where you've been, it keeps you out of trouble."

Apple stared into space, lost in the wonder of it all.

Flustered by his companion's lack of savvy, Slim decided to paint the fool a bigger picture.

"This apple orchard here is in a county, inside a state, inside a country, inside a continent, inside a planet, inside a solar system, inside a galaxy, inside the universe ..." the old man paused. "That is as much as I can tell you."

"Thank you." Apple smiled.

Slim was amazed; here the fellow looked as though he had just been born. He knew nothing about the world, not even where it was.

"So what are your plans? How are you going to sell your merchandise?" the old man prompted.

"Merchandise?" Apple repeated, unsure.

"I used to be a salesman," Slim explained. "You know, your merchandise—who you are, what you do."

"I don't understand."

"In this world are two things you have to do. Being somebody is one, and the other is doing something. Now, human beings can be many things; take me, for example, a homeless drunk, itinerant, what some folks call a bum. That means I travel around and get to see sights for a living. These things you do define who you are, whether you like it or not; but we start with some sort of choice. You see, that's what's beautiful about being human—freedom! It often don't look that way, but you get to make a choice."

"Do you like who you are?"

All at once Slim felt like a fool. Who was he to give advice?

"I made a choice," he said. "You have to make one too, once you find out who you are." He rested his head against the tree and reflected on how and exactly why he didn't like himself. The moment took him by surprise; he stared at the bottle with teary eyes and smiled, seeing a chance to restore his faith in a world he had considered lost.

"Used to," he mumbled, "… used to like myself … you sure this isn't a dream?"

"What is a dream?"

"You never dreamed?"

"I don't know," Apple said truthfully. "Tell me more about it."

"What you see when you sleep, the things you imagine, those are dreams. Sometimes they can be scary. Those are called nightmares."

"I think I'm awake. How about you?" Apple asked the old man.

"I don't know—but in any case, I tell you, this ain't no nightmare," Slim confessed, overwhelmed by long-forgotten joy. He lay down on the grass and breathed deeply. He closed his eyes and concentrated on sunlight filtering through his lids; it warmed his weatherbeaten skin. Many years had passed since he hadn't felt sick without a drink, but the blossoms seemed to embrace him, filling him with their scent. Anxious that all could well turn out to be a dream, Slim cradled his threadbare coat, and keeping his eyes blissfully closed, drifted off to sleep.

II
Rowing for Blue Crabs

The river was only six miles from the apple orchard. The ocean wasn't far, and blue crabs were in season this time of year. They gathered along the riverbank by the thousands, flashing their claws to the sun as they ran backward to the sea.

Theo pulled on clamming boots and climbed into his rowboat, ready to spend the day filling a potato sack with the tasty devils but he was tired. It was a good spot to take a nap. Then he spotted Apple walking along the shore.

"Good morning," he said politely to the stranger. Apple looked deep into Theo's eyes, and sensing great sorrow, he offered him a friendly smile. Prematurely gray from a lifetime nervous disposition, Theo wore a permanent frown that overshadowed his good nature.

"Visiting?" Theo asked, intrigued by the smiling stranger.

"This is a beautiful place," Apple replied, unable to answer the question.

"Sure is. I love this marsh. There's less and less of it everyday … Where exactly are you heading?"

"I'm trying to find something to do."

How strange, he thought, he sounds like he means it. He gave Apple a quick head to toe check and made an on-the-spot assessment.

"Are you planning to stay around here?"

"I think I'll be moving along. I want to see what's up that way." Apple pointed ahead.

"The town is that way," Theo told him.

"Perhaps I can do something there?"

"Theo Andropulos," the man volunteered, waving hello from the boat.

"Nice to meet you. I am Apple."

"That's your name?" Theo looked surprised.

"Slim told me you can call yourself whatever you want."

"That's true," Theo mused, curious about the stranger. Who is this man? he asked himself. Is he a criminal? Can he be trusted?

Theo had retreated with his thoughts to a cabin by the river to get away for the last few weeks. He could use some company. He searched Apple's eyes for a signal or warning, but all he could locate was candor and innocence.

"Are you looking for a job?"

"A job? What is that?"

"Something to do. What you do. That's your job. Do you have one?"

"What I do … to define who I am!" Apple cried.

"Why not?"

Theo digested Apple's words and decided to take a chance.

"Would you like to go catching blue crabs with me? … It'll be fun," he added.

"I don't believe I've ever been on a boat!" Apple exclaimed, delighted.

"Well then, climb aboard."

Apple climbed into the boat and together they rowed to the edge of the marsh where blue crabs seemed to be everywhere. Theo waded in knee-deep and scrambled from stone to stone filling his sack with the peculiar creatures. His new companion stared from the boat.

"They walk backward," Apple observed to Theo, who found the comment naïve.

"That depends on your point of view. It's merely a matter of style. What is backward to us is forward to them," Theo began to explain, but his voice drifted off, along with his gaze. Apple could tell Theo's mind was elsewhere.

"Theo, do you know what you're doing here?"

"What do you mean?" he asked, alarmed.

"I don't know why I am here; do you?"

Theo thought on it awhile and wondered if Apple knew precisely what he was asking.

"… Yes. I come here because it makes me feel good. It reminds me of a better time."

"A better time than this?"

Theo paused and looked hard at the world around him. A band of pelicans glided through the marsh and picked a few crabs for themselves. The morning sun filled the sky. This was a perfect day.

"Right now it's just fine," Theo mumbled. Apple stepped into the water and confronted a crab that challenged him with its claws.

"Have you made something out of yourself?" he wondered aloud.

"Do you think?" Theo bounced back the question, assuming Apple was playing games. "It's a little bit late for that."

"Don't you want to know who you are?" Apple was fixed on the crab, who scuddled around him and hid behind a rock.

"I'm nobody—that's who I am."

"What do you do?" Apple pressed further.

"What haven't I done, is more like it. I've been doing business all my life."

"Slim was a salesman too. He told me about merchandise."

"What merchandise?" Theo asked, shoving a blue crab into the sack.

"You know, your merchandise—who you are, what you do."

"Oh, that." Theo sighed. "I guess I stopped doing that eons ago. I broker securities, commodities and such; I sell other people's merchandise."

"So is there anyone else who can sell yours?"

"No ... I guess there isn't."

Theo was silent. He thought of his bankruptcy and divorce, and how he would not be able to afford another summer here. He thought of his children, who no longer cared, and of his wife, who would not even see him. Thirty-seven years flashed before him, endless meetings and pointless memos coming back to haunt him. Theo stared at the crabs struggling in the sack and empathized with their plight. It had taken them all season to grow, they fought hard to survive and make their way to the marsh to mate—yet here they were, trapped in a bag, failure their only reward. Maybe they too deserved a second chance.

"What do you do?" Theo asked, releasing his catch back into the water. The crabs scurried away.

"I don't know; so far I've met two people and this blue crab, but we haven't been introduced." Apple sat back in the boat. "We should do what we are and be what we do, otherwise we'll never know."

"Know what?" Theo asked, bewildered. "What exactly are we supposed to know?

"Who precisely we are."

Theo smiled, grabbed the oars of the boat, and rowed back up river, thoughts rushing through him like an avalanche. He no longer had use for the gun he had taken to say his farewell to the marsh. Here was only happiness. The day at once felt brand new.

Theo turned to Apple, then turned away, thinking better of putting thoughts into words. He docked the rowboat and the two jumped ashore, where they'd met only hours before. He was surprised to find he was hungry: Theo couldn't remember the last time he'd had an appetite—for anything at all.

"You're a good advisor!" he raved, then he pulled a hundred-dollar bill from his wallet. "Take this for your time."

"What is that?" Apple asked.

"Do you have any money?"

"I don't think so," Apple told him, checking his empty pockets.

"Then take it, you'll need it. I insist."

"Why are you giving me this?"

"It's your reward. You earned it."

"Well then, Theo, thank you." Apple accepted the bill, marveling at its design. "It's beautiful … thank you … very much."

"Where do you live?" Theo wanted to know, intrigued by Apple's honesty.

"I'm living right now. Right here … am I not?" Apple answered, concerned. "Feels wonderful, Theo, doesn't it?"

"Indeed," Theo had to admit.

Apple glanced at his friend, then peered into his eyes. What before looked like distraction now was a calm and peaceful satisfaction.

"I'd like to see this town you spoke of, so I'll be heading that way."

"Sure you don't want to stay for dinner? My house is just up the road."

"Thank you no; I have to find out who I am … so I had better go."

And so Apple headed up river toward town. Theo watched until he disappeared, and spent the rest of his evening staring at the stars, remembering.

III
A Crab's Perspective

On arriving at the edge of the marsh, Apple heard a voice from the shore.

"Big guy!" the small voice cried. Apple decided to have a look.

"Who's there?" he asked to the air.

"Aha! I knew it," the voice replied. "I knew something was different about you!"

Apple looked down and under his feet was the feisty blue crab he'd seen earlier.

"You can talk?" Apple asked, impressed.

"You can hear me! Amazing!" the crab exclaimed.

"Of course. I'm not deaf."

"Hmmm," the crab noted suspiciously. "Where are you from?"

"From here … I suppose," Apple's answer was vague. "Do I look like I'm from somewhere else to you?"

"What's your name?" the little blue crab demanded.

"Apple."

"Exactly what kind of creature are you? I've seen many a human before, and to be perfectly frank, you don't fit the profile."

"I don't?"

"No … No, you don't. For instance, you're standing here talking to me."

"Yet you started the conversation."

"Who are you, really?"

"That's what I'm trying to find out. I'm on my way to town to try to find out more."

"Peculiar! Peculiar indeed," he repeated, sidling in a circle.

"I need to find something to do, so that I can make something of myself."

"What are you now?"

"This is precisely what I'm trying to find out."

"You are long and soft and have fuzzy anemone on top of your head like the rest of the humans do, but all the same, something is entirely different about you."

"Up to now, I've met two other humans—and both were entirely different."

"Don't be silly. Humans are not so different from each other. They live in a world of their own, as if the rest did not exist."

"Really?" Apple sounded surprised. "The two I've met were very nice; one gave me good advice, the other, one of these." Apple waved the hundred-dollar bill.

"I once tried to eat one of those. No good. Don't let looks fool you, at any rate."

"What is it? Do you know?"

"I haven't any idea. Humans carry them in their pockets, inside cowskin beds. They look delicious, don't they?" The crab stole closer and angled sideways, then whispered to Apple in the lowest of tones, "—but seagulls insist that they trade them for fish ... and crabs ... in their reefs near the coast."

"It's pretty," Apple noted.

"And deadly!" He quivered. "Don't you see? I could lose my claws over one of those."

"How dreadful!"

"Dreadful, to say the least! You won't catch me near a rubber band, I try to stay clear of schools. So ... are you a crab eater?"

"Oh ... well, no! Now that I've met you, I guess they wouldn't agree."

"Quite right," said the crab, "we generally don't; it's hard to see eye to eye. So put that away, and if anyone asks, you never knew I was here." The little crab shook and in a trice he covered himself with sand.

"Where did you go? What happened to you? Why did you vanish like that, so soon?"

"Because I'm a crab, and that defines what I do."

"Oh," Apple said to the sand. "People do that, but they do other things, too—to find out precisely who they are. Take me, for instance; I'm heading to town to find out what defines who I am."

"I guess I don't have that problem," said the crab through bubbles. The sand shifted a little, and two eyes on stalks emerged, protuberating toward the back. "I walk that way," the crustacean said, indicating the opposite direction. "That's what I do. It's very simple."

"But human beings do many things—and not all to avoid being seen or to disappear without a trace."

"I do many things too: I open shells, I lay eggs in the sand, I walk across rivers; but mostly what I do is to simply be a crab. Humans may like to complicate things, but in the end, all they are doing is being human—and just like everyone else, they are born, they live, and they die."

"Slim said something about that. You seem to know a lot about humans."

"I've been hiding from them all season."

"They're not so bad, really."

"Says who? You're talking to a crab, mister. Something tells me you don't know much about humans. You must learn."

"I want to learn."

"Then you had better do that before you find out who you are. Otherwise, you may end up thinking you're something you're not."

The crab slid under a rock. Apple thought about what he had heard, and felt more confused than ever.

"Common sense maybe, but being human has something to do with selling your merchandise ..." he murmured half to himself.

"Now you're talking!" he thought he heard the crab exclaim. "That sounds like the kind of mumbo jumbo I wouldn't give three clams about!" the voice was faint now, far away.

The midday sun was above his head. Apple bid farewell to his friend long gone from sight and made his way out of the marsh. He walked for a while until he found a paved road and followed it for some time without encountering a single human being. Not, that is, until he came to a fork in the road, when he saw a vehicle heading toward him.

IV
Dreams When We're Awake

Daisy had her eyes on the road but her mind was elsewhere. First she would pay her bills, then prepare a big bowl of macaroni and cheese for Maggie after picking her up from school. She stared at herself in the rearview mirror. At thirty-three, single, with more wrinkles than ever before and unwanted extra pounds, Daisy felt like a mess. Time, she believed, had not been kind; but she was strong, determined to give her daughter the education she never had, even if it took a thousand bumpy rides in a beat-up station wagon.

The blasting sun was heating up the asphalt, so Daisy cranked up the air conditioning and stepped on the gas. Here near the shore the road became smooth and straight. This was her thinking route. As the car charged ahead, she began to figure in her head the extra minutes she would gain.

Maybe I can take a short nap before lunch or read a little— her thoughts were rudely interrupted by a strange noise from under the hood. Seconds later, smoke shot out from the grille and the engine started to stall. She looked at the panel on the dashboard and everything lit up. She pulled over to the side and popped the hood, unleashing billowing clouds of smoke into the sky. Now she was upset. She kicked the front tire several times and got so angry she turned purplish pink; she would surely be late, her schedule ruined. She looked around. No other cars. The sun was scorching and the tar in the road gave off a wretched scent of rubber and oil.

Daisy sat in the car, furious, wishing she could afford a better vehicle or at least a cell phone that worked. Thoughts of a better car soon turned to thoughts of a better job, a better house—a better life. Pondering these things made her angry, and she felt increasingly bitter and helpless. She closed her eyes and took a few deep breaths. Then Apple seemed to appear out of nowhere. He came toward her with a curious expression, eyes fixed on the vapor rising from the hood. Daisy wondered where the stranger had come from, and why she failed to noticed him earlier. This road went on for miles, nearly all of it straight. The young stranger, however, looked harmless, his surprised expression almost childish; so she decided to think positive for a change and give him the benefit of the doubt. She got out of the vehicle and forced a smile. Apple could tell she was upset; her smile was unable to cover the anger in her eyes.

"I think I've got a hole in the radiator!" she shouted. "I had it fixed about a year ago, but you know how old cars are!"

"I do not," Apple called back. "I do not know anything about cars. Maybe I should," he carefully added.

"Too bad," Daisy said, glum. "Do you have a phone?"

"I don't believe I have one of those."

Daisy found Apple's comments odd and she was a little afraid; she had read horror stories about hitchhikers and she knew this was a dangerous world.

"But the town is that way," Apple replied, "and that is where I'm going. I'd be glad to tell other people. Maybe I can find someone who can stop the clouds coming out of your car."

"The town—it's twenty miles away!" Daisy said, astonished. "I need to get out of here now."

"I like your car," Apple told her. "I've only been on a boat."

Who is this man? Is he for real? Daisy asked herself. Perhaps he was a mental patient who had escaped from a hospital; she couldn't think of any nearby, so she dismissed the idea. Maybe he was impaired and lived with his family somewhere in the marshlands? No, the town was small and she would have heard about him somehow. One thing was for sure—she had never seen him before. The inevitable question poured out, almost unwillingly.

"Who are you?"

"My name is Apple, but I don't know yet. Do you?"

"Do I what?" His question took her by surprise. "Do I know who you are? Of course not, I don't know you," Daisy began, when all at once the stranger felt familiar. "... Do I?"

"Maybe," said Apple. "Do you know who you are?"

"What do you mean? Of course I know who."

"So what do you do?"

"Excuse me?"

"What defines you? Since you know who you are, you must do something, right?"

"Look Apple, I'm not in a very good mood. I need to get back on the road. My daughter will be out of school in less than an hour and no one can pick her up. My day is ruined."

Apple was surprised by the tone in her voice. She was intense and strong; something was bothering her, more than the clouds coming out of her car, something trapped deep inside her. Just then he remembered the crab's advice, to put aside his personal quest and try to understand a human being. He went over to the car and looked at the engine—a marvelous pile of twisted metal. Apple was impressed.

"Human beings make incredible things," Apple observed, fascinated by the pipes and tubes before him.

"What do you call a person who makes these things?"

Daisy found the question absurd, but Apple was so gentle and graceful, she smiled.

"An engineer, I suppose," she offered, reaching for a gallon of water from a bag in the back of her car.

"Do you think one might come by anytime soon?" Apple asked, concerned.

"I need a mechanic."

"What is that?"

"Mechanics fix engines," she explained. "Engineers design them." Daisy opened the radiator by turning the cap and even more steam flew into the sky. Apple was enthralled.

"It has so many pieces." He looked into the engine. "How do all of these work?"

"I don't know," Daisy answered, "I'm not a mechanic." She poured water in where steam came out.

"Human beings can do so many things ... how do people decide what they want to do?"

Daisy filled the radiator and handed the water to him. Apple took a drink and gave her a smile. Could it be possible for him not to know what a mechanic is? Where had he been? She needed an explanation.

Daisy stood next to Apple. He was handsome and although he needed a shave, he had the smell of blossoms. Meanwhile, he could not take his eyes off the engine.

"Human beings know what they want to do because they have dreams," she confided.

"You mean they find out while they sleep?"

"Not exactly," Daisy explained. "I don't mean those kinds of dreams. People have dreams they can see all the time. Not just when they are sleeping."

"What kind of dreams?"

"Of who they want to be, what they want to do."

"That's great," Apple said, excited. "Are you seeing dreams now?"

Daisy paused. Apple noticed her eyes dimmed a bit.

"… I used to."

"Why did you stop? Did you find what you wanted to do?"

"I did—but I realized it was just a dream."

"What about this engine? Wasn't it just a dream once, too? Somebody didn't stop dreaming …" Apple went back to inspecting the engine.

"Not everyone can make her dreams come true."

"Why not?" he asked, fumbling with pipes and hoses.

"I don't know. Some dreams are just that—dreams."

Apple was confused. "Can you make your sleeping dreams come true?"

"Not really; only those you see all the time. The ones you dream when you're awake."

"And you—you … stopped looking?"

"Yes."

"What did you see?"

"I wanted to be the best schoolteacher in the world; but I'll never have time to go to school."

"… But your daughter does!"

"Yes," Daisy said proudly.

Apple gave her answer a great deal of thought. "She must be dreaming hard," he concluded.

Daisy never expected a chill in the midst of a hot afternoon, but there she was under the scorching sun with goose bumps.

"I think the clouds will stay in your car now. Try turning it on," Apple instructed, stepping away from the hood. He looked like a child who just lit a firecracker. She turned the ignition and to her surprise, the engine suddenly started.

"You fixed it! I can't believe it!" she cried. "How on earth did you do it?"

"That tube needed to be in that hole and it was loose," Apple pointed out. "And this band over here was out of place, so I put it back."

"By Jove, you're a mechanic!" Daisy shouted.

"I am?"

"You are!" Daisy looked at her watch. She had exactly thirty minutes.

"That's very good news." Apple seemed puzzled. "Hmm … I've never seen any dreams, though, about being a mechanic."

"I'll give you a ride into town," Daisy said in a rush, "but first I need to pick up my daughter."

"Yes, pick up your daughter, don't worry about me—and don't forget to see the mechanic, who has already done lots of dreaming."

"Are you sure?" she asked, enchanted by his words. "It's rather a long walk."

"I like it." Apple took in his surroundings. "The dreams one has while awake surround us everywhere we look! It's wonderful! I like walking very much."

"My name is Daisy."

"Nice to meet you—I hope you see your dreams again soon." Apple started walking. "Thank you for telling me all about the dreams you see when you're awake."

Daisy opened her eyes. Was it a dream? A few minutes had passed, a few seconds, she was not sure, but the steam was gone.

The Dreamer

She watched the empty road in the rearview mirror and without thinking further she turned on the ignition and stepped on the gas. As her station wagon sped down the road, Daisy started dreaming.

V

The Swimmer Who Saw the Light

The town was a small colonial port that had once been a fishing haven, but those were better days. Its fishing fleet was now reduced to a dozen local ships and a few yachts. Locals survived on the early summer tourist invasion that came to eat blue crab and enjoy the marsh, but by early August the place became a desert. No one dared to go out on the street.

Apple didn't mind the desolate streets; he was enchanted by the charm of it all. The gas station on Main Street instantly attracted him: it was old-fashioned, with two round pumps and a cash register in a small wooden shack. He looked for the attendant but no one was there. He spotted a sign that read BACK IN AN HOUR and tried to remember how long that was. Apple became engrossed, studying the numbers on the counters, feeling the texture of the long rubber hoses and flipping the locks on the handles of the pumps. Human ingenuity never ceased to amaze him.

The smell of gas was making him dizzy, so he decided to head down to the beach. He found a park and sat on a bench and smiled at the sea.

"What a wonderful place to put a bench! Someone must have dreamed this, too."

Down by the shore, Carlos lay on the sand. He was feeling the warmth of sunlight on his eyelids and listening to the waves breaking. The sound was inviting. He felt like swimming.

Just then Apple heard crazed barking. The animal rushed along the edge of the tide while his owner stepped into the sea. The dog was wearing some sort of vest with a handle that dragged in the sand behind, but this did not stop him from charging into the water; he struggled mightily through the foam and swam straight to his master, howling. Apple was concerned.

The man was now far away from shore and swimming even

further. He kept a calm and steady pace but drifted with the current. The dog was following, unable to surpass the breaking waves, but always with his neck above water and eyes riveted on the master. The howling wouldn't let up.

Apple followed them along the shore but did not know what to do—both man and dog seemed fine, and nobody was calling for help. Maybe the dog was telling his master not to go too far, but why? What precisely was the danger? The man seemed a perfectly capable swimmer. Apple saw him turn around and swim straight toward his dog, who yelped and struggled in waist-deep foam. The sea was rough, and it took some time for the swimmer to make his way back; but at last he reached the dog. The animal quickly calmed down and the two headed to shore. The dog led the man out of the water, and Apple found that peculiar.

Together, the duo stopped in unison in front of a pile of clothes on the sand a few yards from the shoreline. Apple was too far away to hear what was happening but figured the dog was in some sort of trouble; the man pointed a reprimanding finger and the dog looked very upset. Apple walked toward them but the man didn't notice; instead, he put on dark glasses and turned his face to the sea. The dog watched without making a sound as the stranger walked up and waved.

"Hello."

"Who is that?" The swimmer spoke with a very calm voice.

"Your dog seemed upset," Apple began. "I think he was worried about you."

"He does that every time I go into the water, but he is not supposed to."

"Hi," Apple said to the dog. "My name is Apple."

The man introduced his canine companion. "This is Ruphus," he said, "and I'm Carlos."

"Very nice to meet you both." Apple smiled at the dog's expression. Ruphus looked at him intrigued; he was a purebred long-haired German shepherd, seven years old, trained specifically for Carlos. Ruphus was as strong as he was smart, and agile; a loyal, majestic beast and the perfect guide for a blind man.

"You can howl very loud," Apple told him. Ruphus simply stared. "Can't your dog talk?" he asked the man, baffled by the canine's silence.

"Just about." Carlos laughed. "He goes with me everywhere I go."

Apple was confused. "Just about?" he asked, incredulous.

Ruphus noticed the disappointment in Apple's eyes and tilted his head the way dogs do whenever they are puzzled. Carlos stroked the fur on the animal's head and breathed the deep sea air.

"Have we met somewhere before?"

"Maybe," Apple replied. "There's a lot about me that I don't know yet."

"Understanding oneself is a difficult job." Carlos smirked. "Hardly anyone does."

"Have you met Theo? He lives near the marsh."

"No."

"He has a boat."

"Don't know him."

"I also met Daisy—an engineer did quite a job dreaming her engine; but the engine is old and clouds came out, so only a mechanic who dreams a lot can fix it now."

"… Those are hard to find," Carlos said, after a pause.

"There is one thing about Daisy I don't understand. She has a daughter who dreams all the time, but she herself stopped dreaming. Daisy wanted to be the best teacher in the world, but she did not have time to go to school. Now her daughter, Maggie, goes to school."

"There are millions of people in this world and hardly any of them can make their dreams come true. The girl is lucky," Carlos explained.

"Oh …" Shocked by the revelation, Apple fell into thought. "But who dreamed of all these things? Who dreamed the engines and hoses and pumps, the cars and boats, the bench on the beach? Who dreamed the town and streets and buildings? Someone had to dream these up. Who, exactly, dreamed them?"

"People with passion." Carlos sighed.

"Passion?"

"Not everyone has it."

"People find out who they are through the dreams they see ... so how can they ever find out if they don't have passion?"

"They simply don't."

Apple looked stricken.

"But don't worry." Carlos smiled. "I think you have plenty."

"Where?"

Carlos laughed and put his hand on Apple's chest. "Inside. You know that engine you're talking about? It runs on fuel; so do you. It's called passion."

"Who would've known?" Apple said, admiring the wonders in his own chest.

"Some people run out of fuel," Carlos muttered. At once he grew quiet and somber.

Apple stood still and tried to process all that he had heard. Getting to know human beings is certainly complicated, he thought. Selling your merchandise, being someone and doing something, seeing your dreams, fuel and passion—a highly confusing ordeal! Apple looked to Carlos and noticed that he always looked to the sea, even when he was talking. What is he looking at? Apple wondered. Is he looking at his dreams?

"Daisy said she stopped dreaming because she realized it was a dream." Carlos listened attentively. "Does that mean that she can't tell the difference between the dreams she has when she sleeps and those she can see when she's awake?"

"Possibly," Carlos whispered, bemused. "Sometimes it's hard to tell."

"How so? All you have to do is wake up and open your eyes."

"Not me ... I can't see with my eyes."

"Oh!" Apple said, surprised. "How do you see?"

"I feel," Carlos told him.

Standing that day on the beach, all of the blind man's senses were peaking; he felt overwhelmed by Apple's presence. Who was this stranger, and why didn't Ruphus make more of a fuss? The dog had never before let him be taken by surprise, particularly by a stranger.

"Don't feel bad," Carlos said with a smile, "I'm used to it."

Carlos had once been passionate, but the years passed by and his dreams changed with him. Life had always been a magical adventure to him. He believed in spirits, angels, and everything else that brought magic to the world. Those were the pictures in his head and they were what inspired his music; for Carlos, this is what brought his fame and fortune. Two years earlier, however, he had heard of a groundbreaking medical procedure: if it worked, it could bring a blind man a taste of light and shadow. Day after day he sat at the hospital praying for a miracle, but six weeks after the last of several surgeries, when the doctors removed the bandages, everything still was dark.

Three months went by, and today, that morning, before walking to the beach with Ruphus, Carlos sat at his piano for the first time in a year—but not one note came. That was the straw that broke him. He felt as though life lost its meaning. Carlos had lost his passion. Even worse, he was getting used to it. Yet a dream stung deep in his soul, even still, a flame filling the darkness; Carlos dreamed of light. That is why he came to this lonely stretch of beach every day to feel the warmth of sun on his face; to imagine what the light must look like.

"You can still see your dreams when you are awake," Apple reassured him.

Carlos needed several moments for the words to sink in. When they did, a smile took him by surprise and the blind musician was overcome by emotion.

"I can," he said, and sitting next to the stranger, Carlos made a tremendous effort to imagine what he looked like. He could hear Apple breathing, he could smell the scent of blossoms off his skin, and most of all, he could feel the pulse of a heart beating next to his; steady and calm as a summer morning.

He kept his eyes fixed, concentrating on his senses, desperately trying to put a mental picture together. The darkness remained but the blind man persisted. Apple was nearer than a heartbeat. Never before had Carlos felt so connected to another human being—especially a stranger—and so he dreamed of a miracle: he dreamed he could see him. Then a marvelous thing happened. The image came first as a silhouette; within seconds the picture was black and white, far from perfect, but clear enough to make his heart beat fast. The first thing Carlos ever saw was Apple's friendly smile.

"So this is what a smile looks like," he said in a joy-filled whisper.

"You must have dreamed very very hard—a spark is glowing inside your eyes," Apple told him, amazed.

"Thank you for reminding me!" Carlos exclaimed, turning to his loyal companion. "Ruphus, I can see you," he said with delight.

Ruphus jumped up, and let out an exhuberant bark.

"There's the sea! Look at it, Ruphus, so big! I never dreamed it would be so big! No wonder you get worried!" Carlos laughed and rushed to the shore. This time the dog did not howl or gallop after his master; instead, he remained seated on the sand and turned to the peculiar human beside him.

"Vat kind of man are you who kan talk to animals and make the blind see? I've never seen one like you," said the dog in a thick German accent.

"I knew you could talk," Apple was quick to respond. "Why didn't you talk to me before?"

"Carlos vouldn't understand. Humans kan't talk to de animals."

"No?" Apple was stunned.

"Nien." Ruphus shook his head as he checked on Carlos, who was now by the shore picking up water by cupping his hands. "Vat did you do to my master?"

"He dreamed he could see. Human beings are capable of incredible, wonderful things. Have you ever seen an engine?"

"I've never seen one dream his eyes back," Ruphus insisted.

29

"I haven't! You must've done something."

"A spark lit up in the black of his eyes, inside; so it had to be a dream."

"You are unique!" Ruphus exclaimed. "You must be careful ..."

"Humans are all unique," he explained. "They dream most everything you see."

"Quatsch! You haven't much been around, have you? Nicht! Not everything dey dream is goot," the dog growled.

"Like the clouds coming out of Daisy's engine!"

"Dat's right, and a goot deal vorse! Have you ever been to de city?"

I don't believe so," Apple replied. "What happens to a person there?"

"Millions of people, like ants everywhere! Dat's vat happens!"

"Millions of people? That's wonderful!" Apple exclaimed. The idea of that many people in one place was exciting. The city must therefore be an immense kind of library.

"You should take a look at de tings dey dreamed of dere," Ruphus told him. "It is a true nightmare!"

"The kind of nightmares they see all the time? Instead of dreams?"

"Richtig," said Ruphus. "Dat's korrect, and dey kan make dem happen, too."

"I have much to learn about human beings and their dreams and nightmares," Apple confessed. "I'd better go to the city to find out more. How do I get there from here?"

"Beyond dose mountains. A loooong vay! Vere de sea is calmed, de road from town vill take you dere," Ruphus pointed out. "You vill see great buildings pointing to de sky—but be careful—and don't talk to animals in public. May get you in trouble mit humans."

"Those are very clear directions," Apple replied, thankful for the advice.

"I'll show de vay, it's vat I do," said the shepherd proudly. "I am a guide, for some."

"I will find out what I do soon enough!" Apple thoughtfully exclaimed, inspired by the dog's determination.

"Achtung! Here comes my master," Ruphus whispered, "Don't forget vat I sed."

Carlos returned from the water puffing, his every breath a celebration. Ruphus barked and wagged his tail, returning to canine behavior.

"Come to my house!" Carlos shouted. "Let's have dinner!"

"I thank you so for your words about passion," Apple told him, amazed by the spark in his eyes. "I can see it is vital to a human's being; but I must be on my way."

"I understand ..." Carlos paused and savored the panorama before him. Graceful waves broke gently in the distance and an ocean breeze cooled the shore. Carlos could not believe his eyes. "Turning belief into fact is a miracle," he said quietly to himself.

"Anything is possible," he said and stared at the sea.

Carlos lost track of time lying under the sun that afternoon but as the tide came in to wet his feet, Ruphus understood it was time to take him home. He licked his master's face as a reminder and Carlos responded with a smile. He stood up from the sand and put his dark sunglasses back on.

" Ruphus, I'm dreaming while awake," he said with great joy. "I've got work to do."

VI
A Sign at the Station

Apple headed back to the gas station with hopes of learning more about engines, mechanics, engineers, and finding the road that leads to the city. He could not stop thinking about what he had come to know about humans and the power of their dreams on the world.

Here, though, was a question he could not answer: If everything is a dream, then who dreamed him?

Deep in thought, Apple arrived at the gas station, where a man sat on a folding chair snoozing while listening to the radio.

"How can I help you?" the attendant asked. He looked different; unlike Slim, Theo, and Carlos, this man's skin was very dark and his hair was braided in neat little strains.

"Are you a mechanic?" Apple asked.

"That's right—I'm the mechanic," the man replied. "Did your car break down? I've got a tow."

"I don't have a car."

"… So what do you need a mechanic for?"

"Do you dream a lot?"

"Say what?"

"Good mechanics need to dream a lot so they can fix the engines that engineers make."

"Hmmm. Sounds like you know a lot about engines."

"Not much," Apple said. "I know engineers dream them but sometimes they break and clouds come out; and a mechanic who dreams needs to fix them."

"I have to agree with you on that … but I never heard it put quite that way. What's your name, stranger?"

"Apple."

"Is that a nickname?"

"My friend Slim says it's very nice; people can pick any name they want."

"That's true," said the man, intrigued by the stranger. "I'm Will, and no, I don't dream a lot. Instead, I sleep like a log."

"What about when you're awake? Aren't you a good mechanic?"

"I'm very good, but no, I don't have those dreams either. I'm thirty-five, and happy where I am."

"Do you have to be unhappy to have dreams?"

"I have ambitions; they're just dreams, that's all ... I ain't gonna let it bother me."

"I don't understand. What do you dream about?"

"When I was kid I wanted to write songs, but I realized some dreams are impossible. What's it got to do with anything?"

"I met Carlos down by the beach with Ruphus, his dog, and he couldn't see, but he dreamed so hard he was finally able to. He told me he could see me."

"He did?" Will looked at him incredulously.

"Yes—you can dream anything you want, and if you dream hard enough, it'll come true. It takes passion—what Carlos calls the fuel for our dreams."

"Are you saying a blind man's cured?"

"I saw a spark in the black of his eyes when it happened—it was passion."

Will did not know what to make of Apple, yet his innocence and his aroma of blossoms made him unlike any other he had ever met; Will was drawn to him. He listened carefully.

"It seems most people aren't lucky enough to have their passion," Apple continued. "Do you think with enough passion you could learn to write songs?"

"You're not from around here, are you?" Will asked perplexed, but before Apple could answer, a pickup truck pulled up to the pumps and an older man in overalls began to lean on the horn.

"Can I get some service? Haven't got all day!" he shouted across the station.

Will didn't say a word. He went to the pump and proceeded to fill the tank. Apple watched the man count the amount and hand it to Will with a dirty look, careful not to touch the attendant's hands. Before the mechanic could even say thank you the man hit the gas and was gone.

"Let me show you something," Will said to Apple. He walked back to his dilapidated office and placed the cash in the register. "You see this?" He pulled up a weather-beaten sign from behind the counter. "I keep it as reminder. It used to be on the bathroom door when I was a little kid."

Apple looked at the wooden sign, intrigued by the words painted on it: WHITES ONLY. "What does it mean?"

"That things around here haven't changed that much."

"I don't understand," Apple admitted, confused.

"I'm a poor black man. Things may look different out there with all them rich white kids dancing, but I am still just that—a poor black man, and nobody ain't handing out winning lottery tickets, know what I mean?"

"Do dreams care about the color of your skin?"

Will was dumbfounded. Was this guy for real? He put the sign down and stared at Apple. "No ... probably not. But men do."

"I don't see why you can't make your dream come true. Maybe you should dream a little harder and forget about that sign."

"Ain't nothing to forget. There's plenty to remember. Did you see that man in the truck?"

"He wasn't very friendly."

"That's Mister Holloway. I've known him since I was little. He hates black folk."

"Why?"

"Because he is a racist. His daddy was even worse."

"What is a racist?" Apple asked.

"Someone who believes that one race is better than another. Some folk think they're better 'cause of the color of their skin or whatever."

"Better?" Apple wondered, "better than what?"

"Better than other people. Some awful things can happen when you start thinking that way."

"They are not dreaming; they are having nightmares," Apple thoughtfully explained.

"And those too can come true," said Will.

Apple was reminded of the guide dog's words. "One must be careful what one dreams," he said, thinking of the warning Ruphus had given him. "But you mustn't let that get in your way."

These words at once struck a chord. Will remembered how he got that sign: Years ago, his daddy used to work for Mr. Holloway's father, who owned the station. When old Holloway, Sr., passed away, Will's dad and uncle gathered all their savings and bought the place. Holloway, Jr., was reluctant about the sale but needed the money. Will remembered the day his father took the sign off the bathroom door and handed it to him.

"This ain't hanging here no more," said his father with a serious look, and he stored WHITES ONLY under the desk, "so that we never forget."

"My father was a mechanic too!" Will said proudly.

"A wonderful gas station," Apple remarked as he admired the pumps.

"The only one around here," Will replied.

"Your father left you that sign to remind you always of his dream."

"He was an honest man."

"Who took the sign off. He had passion." Apple smiled.

"He did, and it took courage, my man. Many people were mad."

"Courage?"

"Yeah, passion's no good without courage. You can't be afraid."

"What are you afraid of?" Apple interrupted. "Your father already took the sign off."

"You're a fast talker, ain't you, Apple man? You one of them foreign exchange students?"

"There is no way to know what kind of person I am

unless I find out more. How much do you know about people, Will?"

"A little more than I know about dreams, but not much," he confessed.

"I'm on my way to the city. I've been told that millions of people live there."

"You've never been?"

"I don't believe so," Apple told him.

"I've never been there either but I've seen it on TV. It's dangerous. What are you going to the city for?"

"I need to study people so I don't get the wrong idea of who I am."

"You wouldn't want to do that," Will said, pausing to count Mr. Holloway's change. It was the only business he'd had all day, but that didn't bother him much; he could feel an itch in the back of his thoughts, a feeling he could not identify—pleasant, profound, healing, and deep, and just as inspiring as the stranger himself.

"I think you've got a knack for fixing things; maybe you helped that blind man see just like you fixed the lady's car. I couldn't tell you who you are, but you're a fixer, I can tell you that. That's your calling, Apple man!"

"You really think so?"

"Without a doubt!"

Apple tried to remember if he had ever dreamed of fixing things, and though he could not, the idea appealed to him. Could it be possible that Apple was doing what he was supposed to be doing already? Yet how, and why didn't he know it? Whose dream was it?

Deep in thought, Apple remembered the blue crab's words and decided to focus on the task at hand.

"I must go to the city," he announced to Will. "I need to learn about people."

"The train station is down the road." Will pointed to a valley behind them.

"I appreciate what you've told me about skin colors and courage. Human beings are complicated." Apple shook Will's hand. "Don't worry, soon enough you'll dream something too."

Will was ecstatic. He couldn't come up with the words, but a smile of gratitude lit his face. Apple waved good-bye and took a few steps before he turned back puzzled.

"One more thing. Would you happen to know, who dreamed you and me?"

"I-I don't have the answer," Will stammered in surprise, caught by the odd question.

"Someone with a good imagination, I bet."

"Maybe you should talk to a preacher."

"A preacher? What does a preacher do?"

"Preachers, they know about things like that, and do they love to talk! He'll tell you all about it!"

"Where do you find a preacher?"

"In a church. There are plenty in the city."

Will returned to his snoozing chair and watched Apple head down the road. A peculiar feeling came over him. He closed his eyes and suddenly he could not recall how long he had been sitting there. A feeling as sweet as the scent of apple blossoms embraced him.

He went into the office and opened a closet where a guitar case lay neglected. He dusted it off, placed it on the counter next to the sign, and opened it with care. Inside was an old acoustic guitar, its cherry wood aged by years of living in a run-down garage. Will's fingers stretched across the neck. He remembered his father's courage.

His song started low and gentle, whispered among trees through the valley.

"Something to remember
Something to live for
To keep up your dreams
Like a sign on the wall."

VII
A Miracle Explained

Apple strolled down the valley toward the train station with sweat dripping down his temples and a head full of questions. Had he truly something to do with Carlos's recovery or Daisy's car coming back to life? He remembered Slim's words — These things you do define who you are —and he wondered whether the events happening around him were trying to tell him something. The blue crab's advice stuck with him, though, and he reminded himself that he had much more to learn about human beings before he could arrive at conclusions.

Theresa sat in her patrol car for over an hour, just like always on late summer afternoons. Parked behind the billboard for Le Blue Crab Restaurant, she often hid there, three miles from the train station. The entire county knew; apart from the occasional local teens too drunk to remember, it was always a speeding tourist who fell into the arms of the law.

Theresa was bored; she could barely stay awake. She slid the car seat back to stretch her legs, and closing her eyes started thinking about how she had once loved her job. Her father had been a policeman, and her grandfather before him. She was only sixteen when her mother died, and she found herself the only child of a brokenhearted cop. Two years later she entered the academy and became the bearer of the family legacy. Theresa's father never imagined his daughter would follow in his steps. Theresa fondly recalled her graduation—the proudest moment in her father's life. She remembered him grinning and saluting from the crowd as the shield was pinned on her uniform.

Crime, however, hardly ever happened in those parts. Theresa would mostly return lost dogs, rescue accident victims, and keep local teens in line. The town had seen three robberies in twenty years, all committed by outsiders; and the only violent crime occurred more than a hundred years earlier, when Jeremiah Stevenson returned from sea and after finding his wife with a man, killed him with a harpoon. Theresa liked to tell this story to tourists asking for directions to Old Jeremiah's Haunted House, a spooky cottage on the cliffs of the north shore. There had been talk of turning the house into a museum.

Her father's recent passing, the museum, the bitterness of the coffee—these were what occupied Theresa while she sat idle in her patrol car. The sun would be down in a couple of hours and deputy Harrington would take over her post; all routine—until excruciating chest pain at once assaulted her. Perhaps the stress she had been through lately, all those late angry nights staring at the ceiling after her father died; or maybe the stiff drinks she gulped every night just to wind down after work; or the six cups of coffee daily? Theresa groped for an answer as she refused to believe that her thirty-four-year-old body would give out on her.

She struggled to reach the radio but the pain in her chest pinned her against her seat. Gasping for air, she opened the car door and her body fell to the ground with a thump. Theresa refused to die. She crawled toward the side of the road in hopes that someone would find her, but no car was in sight, no sign of life; Theresa was deathly afraid. Her chest felt as though it were about to explode and her left arm and leg were paralyzed. To breathe was almost impossible. Her life was flashing before her.

Theresa lay on the ground desperately holding on to her life. She made promises to herself, to God, and to everyone else—but most of all, she told herself she wanted to live. Several seconds passed before she could even take a breath but to Theresa it felt like eternity. Her strength was slipping fast and she could no longer hold herself up; her face hit the ground and she cut her bottom lip. Her vision blurred and the sound of the wind was muffled by her heart's hammering thunder; she feared that in the very next moment, all would be over.

"To Serve and Protect," she tried to whisper but her voice did not respond. Here she was, someone who spent her life devoted to that code, facedown in the dirt, helpless. Who would serve her? Who would protect her? She turned on her back and stared at the sky, convinced that if she kept her eyes open long enough, she would hold on until helped arrived; and so Theresa stayed calm, praying for a miracle, struggling for every breath.

Apple came around a bend in the road and noticed Theresa's body on the ground below the billboard. The metal of her shield flared against a low setting sun. He stood over her and stared at her face. She was smiling. He smiled back.

"I knew you would come," she told him in relief.

"What are you looking at?" he asked, checking the sky himself.

"I did not want to fall asleep," she whispered.

Concerned by the faintness in her voice, Apple searched her eyes. He saw the same spark as in those of Carlos, glowing like a miniature sun.

"I want to live," she pleaded.

"You are alive," he quietly told her. "What is your name?"

"Theresa O'Reilly."

"Mine is Apple."

She felt curiously warm, repeating the name, and the pain in her heart eased a little.

"I can see the spark in your eyes," he said. "It's glowing."

Theresa was taken by surprise. The pain in her chest receded with every syllable he spoke, as though his voice contained magical healing. His words filled her with peace. She felt tingling all over and the world brightened; Theresa was experiencing a miracle. Apple took her hand and everything stopped as quickly as it had begun. She felt fine.

"Help me up," she said to Apple, who knelt beside her. Her arm still ached but all other symptoms disappeared. She took a breath and stared in awe at the stranger.

"Who are you?"

Apple could see the transformation, something unexplainable happened when he arrived. When he looked in her eyes he could see nothing but gratitude, yet what did he do to deserve it? Then he realized he had come at just the right moment, when Theresa was

was dreaming that he would arrive. In some strange way, she had brought him here. She needed him, but why? Why did she show up along his path? There seemed to be no other choice. Perhaps Will was right—that he was some sort of fixer, but it was still too early to tell.

"You said you knew I would come," he said. "May I ask how, exactly?"

"I was praying for a miracle," she said matter of factly, brushing dust off her uniform. Then she looked around.

"Where is your car?" she asked, surprised.

"I'm walking."

"Walking? ... Nobody walks around here ... where are you coming from?"

"The town by the beach. I was talking to Will, who owns the garage. He told me all about courage."

"You walked fourteen miles? In this heat?"

"I'm going to the city. Will showed me the way." Apple smiled at the cop. "You probably know a lot about courage. You need it to make your dreams come true."

"The train station is far." She walked back to her vehicle. "C'mon, I'll give you a ride."

"Your car has a light on it." Apple stared at the siren, greatly curious. "Why?"

"You've never seen a patrol car before?"

"I don't think so. What does it do?"

"It's how a police officer gets around."

"And what does an officer do?"

"We serve and protect," she explained, noticing the strong scent of blossoms. "You never heard of the police?"

"I was in the apple orchard first, then at the marsh, and down by the ocean next to the town where Will has a gas station. Nobody said anything about the police. I'm on my way to the city now."

"How come I've never seen you before?"

"I haven't met many people. That's why I'd like to see the city."

"Hop in." Theresa opened the passenger door. "Don't be afraid—I'm not going to arrest you," she reassured him, joking.

"I bet this car has a very good engine," said Apple, impressed by the dashboard.

"It does. Do you like cars?"

"Human beings dream of amazing things."

Theresa considered herself exceptional at reading people. She could tell an honest person, a thief, an addict, a drunk, or a murderer in half a split second. Police work was in her blood. Yet at that moment she was having difficulty being a cop; her mind was filled with doubt, but her heart was filled by a sense of security she never experienced before.

Where did he come from? Why is he smiling? He smells like blossoms. What happened to me? Theresa's heartbeat calmed with every thought. She stepped on the gas and pulled onto the road.

"What do you do?" she asked.

"I'm learning ... about people."

"Oh, and what do you need to know?"

"Everything there is, I suppose." His tone was childlike and sincere. She took her eyes off the road and looked at him; he was beautiful.

"And why are you doing this?"

"It has to do with finding out who I am. I've learned a few things already ..." he paused.

"Well?"

"It's important to be somebody—and for that, you have to do those things that define who you are: sell your merchandise."

"Hmm," she said, considering. "Is that all?"

He shook his head and continued. "For that you have to dream dreams you can see all the time, and dreaming takes passion—but passion burns like fuel, and people can run out. Then they start having bad dreams they see all the time, and people make those, too, come true."

"People get scared. That's when bad dreams happen. I've seen it done," Theresa told him.

"You're right." Apple thought awhile. "One needs to have courage like Will's father but it's easy to be afraid. Sometimes courage never comes."

"You need more than courage. You've got to have faith," she carefully explained.

"Faith?" Apple seemed perplexed.

"You have to believe. You see, I knew my prayers would be answered. I knew you would come to save me."

"You dreamed very hard."

"You can dream all you want, with passion and courage, but sooner or later you fall down—and getting back up will seem impossible. Just like I felt back there! Lying on that patch of dirt, for a second I thought I was certainly dead; but I had faith. That's where real courage comes from."

"And you had faith that I would come?"

Theresa concentrated on the road, gathering the courage to face her own beliefs. Could this have been a miracle? Why her? Why now—and what for? She did not dare look into his eyes.

"Did you save my life?"

"Your life did not need saving. You are dreaming of living. I see it in your eyes. Maybe your dream was broken and I just came to remind you."

"But how?"

"We all must be part of the same dream, Theresa. The kind someone sees all the time. You believed in that dream; you were expecting me. I think I understand faith."

"I don't know what happened back there … This may sound insane but …" Theresa took a breath. "I'm a cop," she explained. "To Serve and Protect! That's what I do, I'm supposed to be a guardian angel."

"I am glad to have been yours today." Apple smiled.

"So am I," she said as she pulled into the station. "Here we are … the last train leaves in a couple of minutes."

"Take care," Apple said, stepping out of the car, almost as if to remind her.

Theresa waved good-bye. Then she drove straight to the doctor, where she was informed her cholesterol and blood pressure were too high and she was at high risk of having a heart attack. The doctor told her she should eat more fruits, and an apple came to to mind. Not until the ride home did the tears began streaming, and she looked in the mirror and stared in her eyes. She smiled. She was dreaming of living. It was time to wake up to a new life.

VIII
Behind The Glass

The station was a spacious white building. Inside was an enormous single room with tall frosted windows on the sides. A large TV screen showed arrivals and departures, but Apple could not recognize any of the names or tell which train was heading to the city. He looked around for someone to ask but the place was almost empty. A young woman with a baby sat among rows of empty orange chairs that filled the center of the room. She lifted her head and appeared to look right through Apple. He stepped closer and, noticing that the baby was asleep, thought perhaps she was too tired to notice him. The only other person was a redheaded man who sat eyes closed inside a glass booth by the entrance.

"What is he doing in there?" Apple wondered. "What does he need all that glass around him for?"

"How can I help you?" he said through a slit in the glass before Apple could ask any questions.

"Could you tell me which train goes to the city?"

"Which city?"

"The big city," Apple responded, unsure of what name to give.

"That'd be the next one," the man told him, pointing at the empty train platform. "It's on schedule, should be here in a few minutes."

"Thank you very much." Apple headed toward the platform.

"Got a ticket?" the man said through the slit in the glass as Apple stepped away.

"A ticket?"

"Can't get on the train without a ticket."

"I don't have one."

"One way. That'll be thirty bucks."

"What are bucks?" Apple asked with excitement, hoping to make yet another discovery.

"You got any money?"

"Money? Ah! The train, it's just like the crab restaurant, isn't it?" Apple chuckled. "Theo must have known about this," he thought out loud, "and that is what Will gets for gas. Of course! I understand."

"Where are you from?" the man in the booth asked, perplexed.

"I don't really know. I woke up in the orchards."

"Want a ticket or not? I can't give you one unless you've got thirty bucks."

"I have one of these." Apple flashed the hundred-dollar bill Theo had given him. "Is this what you want?"

"That'll do."

Apple handed the bill through the slit. The man examined it in the light, and after being satisfied of its authenticity, placed it in a register beneath him.

How strange, Apple noted; he felt as if the two stood far away from each other, although the man was just inches away. He stared at the glass and came face to face with his own reflection; it occurred to him that if he looked hard enough, perhaps he could see a spark in the black of his eyes.

Apple was deep in concentration when the sound of the ticket being spit out of the machine diverted his attention.

"Gate three," the ticket man muttered and turned back to his newspaper.

Apple looked on confused. He was expecting good-bye but the man behind the glass had no interest at all.

"Why are you behind that glass?" Apple asked as he admired the ticket.

"What?"

"Do you ever go for a walk? You savor all kinds of things. I'm sure you can't smell a thing in there."

"You some kinda nut?" the man asked, provoked, as Apple noticed a peculiar thing: the man appeared to be far away because in fact he was. His mind was in a distant place, even as Apple spoke to him—almost as though the booth were a magic vehicle that transported him to a faraway place. Apple peered into his eyes.

"What are you seeing?"

"What?" the man said, spooked, from behind the safety of the glass.

"Your eyes—they're looking at something not here. Are you seeing dreams right now?"

"Huh?"

"I've never seen anyone gaze that far ... what are you looking at?"

"I'm bored," said the man, taken by surprise, "that's all. Don't have much to look at here. It's the off-season. See that girl? She's been sitting for two and a half hours and hasn't bought a ticket yet."

"Maybe she's got one," Apple said, glancing at the woman in the row of plastic chairs. She looked tired and scared. He tried to look in her eyes but she looked away.

"Nah, I think she's a runaway," the man in the booth continued, "but she's old enough and it ain't my business to be calling the cops. She's got a baby."

"You watch the world from behind the glass."

"I do. Not much to watch, as I said."

"So what else do you see?"

"Ever been to a hobby shop?" the man asked out of the blue.

"What exactly is it?"

"They've got all kinds of toys, like toy trains. They've got lots of hobby shops in the city, but we don't have one around here ..." As he spoke, Apple noticed his eyes growing bright. Something was happening, but what?

"Sounds wonderful," Apple said, thrilled. "Is that what you were seeing—you were dreaming of toy trains?"

"Hey, you're good," he replied in a friendlier tone. "I went to the county fair last year and they had one of them palm readers. She was weird! Anyhow, you kind of remind me of her. I'm Luke. Very nice to meet you."

"Hello, Luke. I'm Apple. So what are you doing in a glassed-in box dreaming of toy trains?"

"I've got money in here!" he answered, sliding Apple's change through the slit.

"And … ?"

"Apple you say, right?"

"Yes."

"Did you just fall from a tree or something?"

"I don't know. Have you met anyone who fell from a tree before?"

"I did. But I broke my arm."

"I seem to be fine." Apple quickly inspected himself. "Tell me more about the glass and money."

"You tryin' to pull a fast one?" Luke slid away from the glass. "I'll tell you now, mister, it ain't worth the trouble. It's been a slow night! Besides, this is bulletproof"—he tapped the thick pane—"it protects me against robbery."

"I think money comes from working," Apple told him. "That's what Theo says; and that's what the man who doesn't like Will gave him for his gas! I had a job. I went to the marsh with Theo. He threw all the crabs back in the water and gave me the money I gave you. It worked out well for everyone; Theo is happy, and the crabs don't have to worry because the hundred-dollar bill isn't going to the restaurant."

This guy is insane, thought Luke. So why am I talking to him? The question itched in his head. Not too many people stopped to speak to him, and up to now, he liked it that way.

"No one's here and it's early yet so I suppose I could take a short break," he said. He hung a BACK IN FIVE MINUTES sign on a hook attached to the glass.

"Do you live in the city?" Luke asked Apple as he let himself out of the booth.

"I don't believe I've ever been there," Apple replied, "I'm on my way to learn."

"Hmmm …" The ticket agent looked doubtful and headed to the main rails. "C'mon, I'll take you over to the platform. I need to stretch my legs." He walked quietly across the station so as not to disturb the girl with the baby. They reached the platform and Luke gazed at the tracks stretching into the distance.

"It's safe behind the glass," he confessed.

"The air is nice out here." Apple stopped to take a breath.

"But dangerous, nevertheless."

"You must have courage to take your dreams outside of your glass box."

"Easy for you to say."

"You know what I've learned so far?"

"From who?"

"From people," Apple replied.

"Go ahead." Luke smirked in disbelief.

"We need to make something out of ourselves. People need to find out who they are so they can be best at being themselves. Yet we already are something; most of us don't know what that is right away, but we need to find out to be true. The only way to do that is through our dreams—the kind we see when we're awake. Dreams like those you have in the booth. "Everything you see is one's dream: your booth, this place, and even the trains at the hobby shop. Even then, not everyone can make a dream come true, so some never find out who they really are! You need to have passion—the fuel that drives us—but also courage, because at times the fuel runs out and we're afraid. Then, even courage has to come from somewhere; that is when you need faith—you need to believe. It's complicated and I'm sure there's more ..."

"What if you have nothing left to believe in?" Luke muttered. "Where does the courage come from?"

"You have nothing to believe?" Apple asked, surprised.

"Not really," said Luke, "I don't."

"So why are you seeing dreams while you're awake?"

"When did you start thinking these things?" Luke asked, trying to avoid the issue.

"It started with Slim, and—" Apple broke off, then asked with enthusiasm, "—have you ever seen an engine?"

"Here comes one now," Luke said, excited. Apple saw the spark return to his eye—the same he had seen earlier, hidden deep. The ground beneath their feet started to shake and the train appeared in the distance, charging toward the station at cruising speed. Apple was enthralled by the new sensation as the colossal engine hit the breaks and screeched its way to the platform.

"An amazing dream," he said to himself, "a mighty big dream that is!"

In that moment, as the train rolled in—a cacophony of sliding metal and chuffing hydraulic sounds—Luke looked like the happiest man in the world.

The doors opened and no passengers came out. A tall man in a blue uniform jumped onto the platform and the locomotive came to a stop. Luke watched with keen admiration as the man hopped from the engine like a cowboy off of his horse.

"That's the conductor! He's just taking a break. The train will be leaving in precisely five minutes. I better get back in there." Luke turned to Apple. "So long. It's a pleasure to meet you."

"You dream of being a conductor," Apple said in parting.

"I like trains," the ticket man murmured.

"This is your dream and you've been dreaming it a long while. You do have something to believe in, don't you? ... But you don't want to tell me—you don't want to believe—you're afraid."

"You have a gift there, Apple," Luke admitted. "You know people well. But I'm too old, and my life ain't that bad. No one bothers me behind the glass and I can listen to any radio station I want ..."

"But you do believe you could be a conductor."

"No, not really," Luke told him fairly.

"So why do you dream it from behind the glass?"

"I like my job," Luke assured him. "People can't give me their colds in there. Except for Christmas three years ago, when I had a coffee with some guy, this is the only time I've come out of the booth to talk to a customer—you want to know why? Because people are evil! They're cruel, unkind, they let each other down; and they'll rip your soul apart if you let them. I want nothing of people." Luke was upset; his cheeks turned pink and his hands went deep in his pockets as though he were restraining a maddening rage.

"I do believe it," Apple responded, "wherever I am, I'll believe in you and your dreams. I'll see you as a conductor, and you'll be part of my dream and I'll be part of yours because now we both know who you are."

"You're nice," Luke said without a smile, "good luck in the city. Go ahead. Don't be late for the train."

Luke returned to the booth, shut the doors tight and sat quietly on his chair. The conductor headed to the train without ever glancing back. The girl with the baby was no longer there.

The station was empty. He leaned forward and rested his head against the glass to peek at the train still at the gate. The engine started once more, and the familiar whistle marked its departure. Luke tuned the radio to one of his favorites. He wanted to cry but pride made him reluctant. He pretended this was just another day, indeed, another day behind glass; the idea terrified him.

The train pulled out with rolling thunder and Luke realized inside there was at least one person who would believe in him. One capable of seeing into his soul and seeing the dream he'd forgotten. Maybe humanity is not all cruel, he thought. Maybe I made a friend today, and if a stranger can believe in me, why can't I believe in myself?

Luke made an effort to quiet his thoughts but a memory came to pierce his shell, armed with layers of emotions. Something deep inside him persistently refused to remember a small detail—one about four feet tall who played with trains, the one with dreams. Luke thought he would never see him again but there he was, reflected in the glass, a gift from a stranger who smelled of blossoms: Little Luke, the Conductor. Choo Choo, he remembered the sound of the train. He was no longer safe behind the glass; his dream had come for him.

And Luke wept. At that moment, he opened his eyes and realized that perhaps he could still buy a ticket.

IX
The Corner Seat

The train car was filled with passengers, but Apple sensed an uneasy emptiness: people were involved solely in what they were doing, whether reading, listening with earphones, or staring at propped-open screens; no one paid attention to anyone else. Apple walked unnoticed down the aisle. This was a lonely world.

How easy it is to feel like Luke when nobody notices anyone else. He found an empty corner seat at the tail-end of the car. He sat quietly contemplating the back of people's heads, hoping for a face to talk to, but not one of them turned around. How interesting, he thought, just like Luke's glass, these props serve much the same purpose—to keep one distant from the nearest other. But why? Apple wondered. Do they know who they are already, having made their dreams come true—or is each of them hiding, like Luke?

A crank, a hiss, and a jolt marked the beginning of the journey and the train lurched forward. For Apple, the experience felt brand new. He could not recall ever being on a train before and found the sound of metal wheels accelerating on tracks exhilarating. He smiled broadly but no one noticed.

The train rolled through open fields until the landscape became transformed into a world of man-made dreams. Bridges and highways hummed with cars, large buildings with stacks spewing steam into the sky, and billboards selling things that Apple didn't understand—Financial portfolios, HMOs, and little white sticks called cigarettes.

These things must have something to do with people being happy, he guessed, gazing at the smile-crazed faces pasted on the signs. An hour went by and Apple's eyes were glued to the world outside. The train eventually slowed and came to rest in the station. He watched all the passengers disembark, hoping to find that spark in someone's eye, but nobody looked at him. He took note of a woman's tired expression buried behind a big pair of glasses; two girls bopping their heads to the music as they giggled down the platform; an older couple dragging their suitcases and spilling chips to the delight of the pigeons; and three young men of different skin color wearing similar uniforms and the same stern expression. Apple was enraptured. If this many people were in one train, how many would be in the city?

Human beings come in all shapes and colors, just like their dreams, Apple observed. Some like Will, others like Slim, Carlos, Theresa, and Luke—all come in shades of human; but is it possible they travel in their own glass boxes?

The conductor was resting on an empty seat between stops. He got up and entered the car, ready to do his passenger count, when he heard a voice that startled him.

"Hello!" Apple piped from the corner seat behind him.
The conductor turned with a snap and discovered a ticket he had not punched. He grabbed it and made his formal announcement.

"Last stop, next," the conductor said quietly, realizing the car had emptied but for the lone young man. That corner seat had been giving him trouble ever since it was first installed. The seat had no integrity; it was hidden next to the exit door, and because it abutted the bathroom, it went against rules of good service. He looked Apple straight in the eye and handed him back the ticket.

"Last stop, next! The city," he said. "We should be there in about twenty minutes ... that is where you're going, isn't it?" The conductor sensed that Apple was a stranger to these parts—for one thing, he was smiling.

"Yes," Apple answered eagerly. "Where are you going?"

"Home, as soon as my shift is over," the conductor said, finding the question odd. "Are you all right?" He appeared concerned.

"Of course—I can't wait to get to the city. I'm excited to meet more people. It's a pity everyone was so quiet in here."

"Yes, well, er ..." The conductor seemed slightly flustered. "Well ... good luck," he said when the train started moving.

"I think I understand," Apple told him as he walked away. "While the train is in motion we must act like we're behind glass ... but Luke was dreaming, unlike the passengers here," he noted. "Perhaps it's because no one would let me see their eyes. What do you think?"

"Pardon me?" the conductor asked, stopping cold.

"I notice how everyone keeps to themselves; well, Luke dreams of being a conductor, but he spends all his time in a glass box instead—and in it, he goes to a place far away. The people here, too, were all very quiet; they don't seem to see one another."

"There was a time when riding a train was exciting," the conductor reminisced.

"It's exciting to me!" Apple quickly responded.

"Is that so? You really like trains?"

"Probably not as much as Luke, but yes, I like all dreams! I especially like meeting people who dream them—it's the best way to learn about being, well, human."

"I've got to agree with you on that one." The conductor smiled, charmed. He felt transported to a time when trains had lovely waitresses in dresses tending the aisles; when a polite passenger was not the exception, and every new face was a friend. "How times have changed." The conductor sighed.

"I've been doing this job for thirty-two years and that's what I've always loved—the people. You get your regular commuters, but always a fresh face in the crowd. Like you. I didn't notice you before because I forget about this corner seat. It's hidden there and … anyhow, I'm Owen, what's your name?"

"Apple, picked the name m'self."

"That's a new one! Are you a student?"

"A student … yes, at the moment. I study human beings. I'm interested in the dreams they have—that is, when they're awake."

"Aha! A psychology major, or something along those lines?"

"I don't know. I need to find out who I am."

Apple had a tone of sincerity Owen found rare. Where's this kid from? he asked himself. "Do you live in the city?"

"My first time," Apple told him with excitement.

"Is that so? Er, well …" Owen was speechless; he took a moment to think. Apple was a lamb about to be fed to the lions.

"People don't have time to pay attention—or even less to care for somebody else. That's what you noticed here today. It's a crime.

They have a choice ... Sure Luke's got a dream inside that booth, the streets are filled with dreamers! But they're afraid of each other, they just try to survive. We trap ourselves inside our worlds, that's what life has become. It's lived behind that glass you've seen—but it's a choice! It's safety glass."

"Slim said we all start with some sort of choice," Apple responded. "I think it's dreaming. The dreams we choose are up to us."

"You keep talking of dreams; what do you mean?"

"The dreams you dream when you're awake. Those that can come true." His words took Owen by surprise.

"Ah ... those," Owen murmured, and in a flash, his life began to add up—almost as if by magic.

"There it is." Apple smiled. "The spark in your eyes!" This was his favorite part about talking. "How does it feel?" he asked with a grin.

"How does what feel?" Owen replied, unsettled by emotion.

"To know who you are. To see a dream come true."

A long time had passed since Owen paid any attention. He was sixty and had spent the last thirty years trying to make others' dreams come true. His life had been far from fancy, scored by the sounds of screeching metal, power horns, and obstreperous children. Punching tickets and filling out schedules while raising a family on weekends never seemed a successful life, but Apple's question put a new spin on things. All those ballgames, barbecues, movie nights and birthday wishes, presents under the Christmas tree, Father's Day cards and graduations, the births and hugs and kisses, all the sacrifices, all the rewards—all those memories piled up in Owen's heart like irreplaceable treasure. He had done much dreaming in his life and it had taken this long for him to see: all his dreams had come true.

"It feels ... great," the conductor whispered.

The train slowed down and Apple looked out, amazed. As the buildings grew taller in clusters, the green of trees and deep blue of sky glinted through the structures.

"We're almost there. I should finish my count," Owen said, reluctant.

Apple rose from his corner seat. "Thank you, Owen, for telling me all about the safety glass."

"Take care of yourself … and thanks!"

The train came to a stop and Apple stepped off, disappearing through the exit.

"Apple," Owen shook his head. "I was wondering when someone would fill that seat." He laughed the laugh of a lucky man who would never again take something for granted.

X
The Flock

By the time Apple walked out of the train station it had started to drizzle. The city was overwhelming. Apple stood lost among the pulsing beat of thousands of feet, blaring horns, the roar of planes, and strange new people. He thought about what Owen told him—people having no time to pay attention or care for somebody else—and realized he was on his own.

Apple considered what to do next. He remembered what Will said, that "preachers love to talk." So he decided now was as good a time as any to visit a church and ask a few questions, specifically about the Dreamer.

The young crow noticed the figure from a third-floor balcony, where he was stealing food from a poodle's bowl. Crows are highly intuitive, and this one got an eerie feeling, the kind he felt before a storm—only something was guiding him toward it, rather than away; whatever it was, he could not resist. Curiously, it was neither in the wind nor in a scent from the South nor in a piping-hot plate of spaghetti. This message was different—it came from a man—and to the crow, held even more fascination than the sun. Who could this human possibly be, when all of his senses were ringing like bells?

"He doesn't appear to be much of a threat," the young crow croaked, suspicious. With that in mind he flew down to the steps to get a better look at the oddity. Apple spotted him instantly.

"I am new here," he spoke to the crow. "Do you know where I can find a church? I need to talk to a preacher."

At first the crow thought it was a trick, just like the plastic owls. Was this another human trap, a vile attempt to terrify his kind? The human expected an answer.

"You can tell me," Apple spoke again, "no one is listening but you."

The crow played it safe. He hopped a few steps toward Apple and stared into his eyes.

"Human beings dream a lot of things," Apple began to the crow. "By the looks of it, they may be running out of space; so I'm wondering, exactly who dreamed us?"

The startled crow held his gaze.

"My friend Will said I should talk to a preacher. He tells me they know of these things. You live here, don't you?" Apple persisted. "You must know where a temple is."

This was an unnatural act. Dangerous forces were certainly involved. The crow recalled the time he tried to get a chicken leg out of a truck and almost got crushed by a yellow jaw—so he decided to call for a second opinion.

"*Caw! Caw!*" he screamed. They flew from rooftops and garbage cans, across traffic and through antennas; within seconds the entire flock was there, all nine of the glossy black birds.

"What do you make of this, guys?" the young crow asked the others.

"Hello, fellows!" Apple saluted them. "I just arrived and I need directions."

A tallish crow hopped toward Apple and demanded some facts.

"What type of creature are you? You are most unusual." He eyeballed the intruder.

"I'm a human being," said Apple.

"Go back to wherever you came from!" cried the crow. "You don't belong here."

"Why not?"

The crows looked at one another confused, hoping their communal instincts would provide an answer, but the flock was lost. All they could gather was an unsettled feeling.

"Because you're talking to us," the tall crow stated.

"Why shouldn't I understand you?" Apple replied. "A guide dog warned me that humans would be afraid if they knew I could talk to animals, but Ruphus told me nothing about birds."

"Crows!" the tall one corrected him. "We're not just any birds, we're crows."

"We're the smartest there are!" The young one strutted in pride.

"And you're in our neighborhood," another complained.

"That's right," the rest of them gabbled in unison.

"Better leave. Before you start any trouble," suggested the tall one.

"I'm trying to find out who I am," Apple informed the group, "but I need to know more about being human first."

"First you should know that humans don't talk to crows. You shouldn't be here, you've lost your path; now leave our flock at once. Remember where you went astray. Then you'll find your way."

"We know all about finding things!" the young crow added. "We can go over fifteen hundred miles for corn!"

"I'm human too, like the rest of these people," Apple said, getting back to the subject. "I just don't yet know who I am. Perhaps my flock is close nearby, if I could only find them."

"Human beings know only packs, they're even more treacherous than rats—"

"—much more dangerous even than hawks and owls!" the young crow interjected.

Apple gestured around him. "All these human beings are dreamers, but each is afraid of the others. They hide behind glass, believing that by caring only for themselves will they ever be safe ..." Apple looked up, then down at the crows. "This is why only those who dream outside the glass when they're awake ever make their dreams come true. Have you ever seen an engine? Look at all these things"—he raised his arms to the buildings—"these are amazing dreams! These are why I want to find out who dreams us; it may explain everything."

"Listen carefully, Crow Talker," the tallest and wisest bird said. "I am already breaking the code of nature by speaking to you, so I will tell you what a crow knows: the great feeling flies with the wind and it burns in the sky; it grows from the ground, falls from the clouds, and beats in all hearts. We are here one moment and there the next, but the great feeling is everywhere. You can feel it, hear it, even see it if you pay attention; but only animals know this, especially the crows—that is why humans fear us, because they sense we know something they don't."

"Are you saying there is one dreamer who dreams it all?" Apple asked with a glimmer of joy.

"There is one great feeling," the crow assured him. "That with which you are one. This is why we flew to you—your kind attacks what it does not understand; you don't belong here."

"I'm trying to learn more," Apple whispered. "I believe we are all one with great feeling."

The smaller birds fluttered. "When you find out more about humans," one of them exclaimed, "you'll question the intention of whoever dreamed them!"

"Guaranteed!" another volunteered.

"Oh, I've heard about the bad dreams," Apple responded, "but not everyone has them. Human beings have a choice."

"A choice of what?" the crow wanted to know.

"They can choose whether or not to dream from behind the safety of the glass. They make that decision," Apple explained. "You, however, are crows: you know who you are and you do what is right from the get-go; human beings don't. They have to make choices, and if they are right, they get to find out who they truly are—and that's when good things happen. This is why I must find out who I am. So I can dream the right thing. I don't yet know just who I am, but I'm sure that whoever dreamed all this does; maybe if I hear what the Great Feeling has to say, I can find out what kind of dream I am."

The crows were speechless. The stranger was right. No crow ever took itself for a duck. They know how to do things the way they do, with no chance for mistakes.

"The great feeling does not speak," the tall crow said after a lengthy silence, "but you are different. Maybe you will hear it. Go that way," he directed Apple, pointing through a maze of buildings at a sliver of horizon. "You will find the pigeon's nest. You cannot miss it: the building with a tower in the center. Hundreds of birds will be there."

"And don't bother talking to them, they're all extremely dumb and dirty." The young crow preened his feathers. "And they only care about one thing—"

"Enough!" cried an old crow, cutting in. "You'd better get away from here and stop talking to us," the bird warned Apple, "before they take you away in cuffs, like they did to the silver crest man."

"Who is he?" Apple pressed, reluctant to go.

"He was old, and he used to talk to us too; he brought us food every day. But then one day the stickman came and tried to take the food away. The silver crest got so upset the great feeling left his body—and all at once he fell broken to the ground."

"They took him away in their howling car with flashing lights on top," added the younger crow. "It was awful, awful!"

"Stickman has been after us ever since." The tall crow bristled.

Inside the station, George, the so called "Stickman," hid from the world in the broom closet. It was dark and quiet in there and the stench of ammonia stung his nostrils but he did not mind, it was a perfect retreat for visiting faraway galaxies. He closed his eyes and remembered all the wonders he had seen through his telescope. It brought a smile upon his face. Yet all of a sudden he got that awful feeling. It was almost as if he had a built-in radar to detect his enemies, and it was buzzing in every inch of his being. It was his nightmare haunting him again, ready to destroy him. George remained stern.

"Not this time," he said to himself. The city was outside cruel, cold, and oblivious to his pain. "Why risk it all?" he asked, but he could not resist the impulse.

"This is a dangerous place," the elder crow said to Apple, "go now!"

"I appreciate all your help," Apple told the crows. "I'll be sure to look for the birds in the tower."

All at once, as if they'd heard thunder, the flock leaped into the air.

"Here he comes!" shouted the young crow, "and he has the stick!"

61

"To the roofs!" shouted the leader. "Fly away! Go! Before you fall broken to the ground!"

Apple watched astonished as the flock flew up in unison and disappeared above the buildings.

"Were you feeding those birds?" George's voice came from behind him. He was wearing a gray uniform and held a broom and a big plastic bag. "Because if you were," George continued, "I'll call the cops on you. Were you talking to those things?"

Apple took the crow's advice and quickly changed the subject; he pointed to the distance and offered a smile.

"Is the church that way?"

"I don't know, I don't go to church," the janitor answered with a frown. "There is no feeding the crows."

"Oh, but I was not!"

"You were talking to them," George accused.

Apple wished to tell him the truth but thought it best to keep quiet- to give him the benefit of the doubt. So he looked into the angry man's eyes to see how far behind glass he was dreaming.

"What are you looking at?" George demanded.

"The crows are afraid of you," Apple confessed.

"They ought to be, the scavengers!" He cursed, then gave Apple a questioning look. "Are you lost or something? I see you talking to birds, in the rain without a suitcase."

"Do I need a suitcase?"

"I don't know," George responded, "that's your problem."

"I have money," Apple told him, showing him the change Luke had given him back.

"Put that away," George said, alarmed. "You don't flash cash around in the city. You're going to get robbed."

"Luke told me about robberies." Apple folded the money. "That's why he works behind safety glass. What is your name?"

"George … I'm the janitor," he said, none too happily.

Apple couldn't help but notice. He looked deep once again, as he always did, for the spark in the janitor's eyes, but George was an impenetrable wall.

"You dream of being something else," Apple told him at last.

George found the comment peculiar. What did his dreaming have to do with the crows or his being a janitor? Could this fellow be insulting him?

He locked eyes with Apple, spoiling for a fight, but instead he got a welcoming feeling. Nothing was strange about the stranger; in fact, he was all too familiar—as though he were a brother or prodigal son. George never before felt this way about anyone he'd met in the city.

In that moment, George scanned the buildings for his winged archenemies when he remembered an important detail: the dreaded birds never flew out in the drizzle. Why had they come down this afternoon?

"Yes ..." George answered cautiously. "I'm an astronomer ... I study the universe ..."

"That's big! My friend Slim explained it to me," said Apple. "Infinitely big!"

"Indeed," George agreed.

"Who do you think dreamed it all?"

George didn't answer. He stood on the steps in silence.

"If people can dream these things"—Apple pointed to the city around them—"and make it all come true, then how do we come true? Who dreams us, exactly?"

"Life is a mystery," George mused, remembering the days before the war. In his homeland he'd been a scientist, observing galaxies and stars from inside a dome of glass and steel. Now that was over and done. His family had scattered around the world, and those few who survived were barely in touch. Some had gone East, others West, but all were strangers in a foreign land. It had been a long time since George felt at home—even longer since he hadn't felt alone. Apple was a reminder that he wasn't the only one.

"I don't know much about dreams," George confessed. "I can't sleep at night, I got in trouble at work because I'm so tired... so I don't dream much."

"What about dreams you see when you're awake?"

George had never pondered such things, yet he knew he had plans: to save enough money with his janitor job to bring his sister over from his homeland. He also had goals: to get married someday and work at a great observatory. Plans and goals they were indeed, all carefully designed and archived in the halls of his ambition, fueled by need and sacrifice. His small apartment, his exile, his loneliness—all had become the prison he called his life, and he was making plans to escape it. George had never pictured his plans as dreams before, not until that moment.

There had been many complaints about "the crazy janitor who swings a broom at the crows." Local vendors warned the train station manager that George could possibly injure a passerby, and the police department had also issued a warning; but he didn't care. He had to get rid of those birds.

George planned to make telescopes someday. So far, he'd managed to save enough money for one year's tuition but his plans had come to a halt—all on account of birds. After two years of cleaning their mess, George could take it no longer; he suffered a nervous breakdown. It had started several weeks earlier, when he finally lost his temper and the old man fell on the steps.

That Friday, George had just finished the steps and was getting ready to punch out when the old man arrived with his box of nuts. George knew what would happen next. Rushing first to the utilities closet, he then charged outside, raising his broom like a pillaging barbarian. The flock of crows shot into the sky with an explosion of feathers. The old man was given such a fright that he dropped to his knees and rolled down the steps. An ambulance raced him to a hospital and minutes later he was dead. The old man had had a heart attack and could not be revived.

George felt terrible. He had not been able to get much sleep and the feeling was getting worse. Day and night he was obsessed with fighting the crows and he was so exhausted he had been found napping twice in the broom closet. Just that morning, only minutes before spotting Apple in conference with his enemies, George had been given an ultimatum by the station manager. "One more time," he was sternly warned, "and you will be fired!"

In short, the birds had ruined his life. Those devils hadn't come around as much since the old man's "accident" and when they did, it was only one or two at a time. So when he saw the entire flock, he ran at them with his broom in a desperate attempt to exact his revenge.

"I dream to be a telescope operator," George answered at last. "I wish to discover a new star someday and to give it a name."

Apple did not remember what a telescope was but he was enthralled with George's expression.

"I've always dreamed it. All my life," George told him.

"So why are you sweeping up with that broom?" Apple demanded. "You know exactly what to do, don't you?"

"… I'm all alone here in this city … it's going to take me a while …"

"A conductor named Owen explained to me that people are afraid of each other; that's why they live inside themselves, behind the safety glass."

"That's probably true," said George, feeling as if he too were hiding in his prison. He smiled at his own reflection in a window across the street: alone in the crowd, his mirror image stood on the steps by itself. The world, blurred with movement, swirled around it, oblivious. His eyes turned to the sky and he noticed a star.

"It's hard to see stars in the city," said George. "You can only see one, but they're all around us."

"Just like people," Apple noted, "and dare I say, the crows."

George looked all around him. People's expressions weren't unfamiliar; they hurried through the drizzle grabbing taxis, lining up for buses, or getting lost in the crowd. The sounds of trains, the scent of vendors, nothing out of the ordinary. So why did he feel so strange?

"This is a very lonely place," George confessed to Apple. Yet here he was, engaged in conversation with someone who talked to the crows—again. It was the last thing he expected. Maybe, he thought, this was a second chance, an opportunity to redeem himself. At that instant, his expression softened, and his eyes opened wide enough for Apple to see. There it was, the spark—glowing in his pupils like a freshly lit torch; and not behind safety glass. It came out and blossomed into a smile that even George couldn't explain.

"What are you seeing right now?"

A simple question, for which George had countless answers: you, that woman crossing the street, the ad on that taxi, that man's shoes, the old man's hands, the color of her hair, the woman in the third-floor window; all was happening in unison, and he could see it all as if staring into a galaxy through his telescope. All had become one thing.

"Everything," he whispered and took a step back to check if the crows were still on the buildings. They weren't. The entire flock had flown away. How could it be? They had been there all summer. Making that horrible sound, hustling food from people, scavenging on the steps of the station like beggars, and now they were all gone.

Then, from out of nowhere, the birds appeared and landed before them. The tallest bird hopped forward, and fixing George with a stare, he croaked—but not without a meaning.

"Did you hear that?" George's eyes were agog. "Did that crow just say something to me?"

"Everybody belongs—this is the big city!" Apple sought to make him understand. "This is their home as much as it is yours."

Home was a word George held dear to his heart. Home was what he was missing, and the feeling he missed the most. His overstuffed apartment didn't qualify, nor did the city itself.

"I haven't any friends. No family, no home," he explained to Apple, almost as an apology; "just this job, just this dream. I don't mean any harm."

Facing the flock of crows and a most unusual stranger, George smelled the scent of blossoms; it reminded him of home.

"This is a very lonely place, this home of ours," George said to the crows, ashamed.

"But you have a choice," Apple responded. "You are a human being."

George listened to Apple and looked to the crows; they were staring at him like a jury. No longer able to contain himself, he fell to his knees.

"I'm sorry!" he wept to the flock. "Did you hear what it said?" he turned to Apple. "Did you hear what that bird said to me?"

Apple was moved. He could feel George almost as if they were one, the man a fountain of emotion. He needed someone and he'd found him. His tears were tears of relief.

Apple then understood what he hadn't known before: a need for something behind the dream. Slim needed a sleeping buddy; Theo needed help with a boat; Daisy needed someone to fix her car; Owen needed a smile. "One Dream," he thought "we are incomplete without each other because we are part of one dream." It was a revelation.

"Did you hear what it said?" George kept repeating.

The crows inched forward, closer to George, until they were at arm's length. George stopped moving, but he wasn't afraid. Instead, he looked into the tall crow's eyes.

"Do you forgive me?" he begged the crow.

An intrepid young bird leaped up and landed on his shoulder with a flutter.

"You have found a flock," Apple told him, and George began to laugh. He stood up and looked at the bright star above him, just as the crows took leave. Within seconds, their silhouettes disappeared into shadows, then vanished.

"Good luck to you," George said to Apple and watched silently as the young stranger walked away and disappeared amongst the pedestrians.

George locked the doors of the broom closet that day to never return, it seemed like the stars guided him all the way back to an observatory, but he never forgot that day when the crows flew down from the sky to tell him;

"Welcome Home, George!"

XI
Brokenhearted Mary

Apple had been walking for several miles but could not stop thinking about the moment when George became one with the Great Feeling—as though a part of him were missing and something had completed him and he was set free, never to be alone again.

Apple was convinced that there was a lot more to dreaming than he had suspected; what was this Great Feeling, and where did it come from? Is it the cause of our dreams? The Dreamer itself? Or is Great Feeling merely the language of the Dreamer? He would be arriving at the pigeon's nest soon.

Engrossed in his surroundings, Apple was thrilled by the lights and invention of the city. A vast boulevard flickered in neon rainbows that shimmered along the asphalt. He was hypnotized by it all. Looking around, his gaze fell upon a small wooden sign propped up on the sidewalk in front of a building. The sign was plain and slightly faded, with weatherworn words that held an irresistible appeal: YOU ARE A MIRACLE—YOU ARE UNIQUE, and underneath those words, framed by a pair of magical hands, MARY THE FORTUNE-TELLER—$15.

A scent of sweet perfume escaped from the open door of Mary's humble establishment. Apple found it inviting and decided to peek inside. The room was purple and jammed with objects: candles and burning incense, statues and paintings everywhere, and in the back, a tall velvet chair that faced a small couch next to beaded curtains that led into another room. A welcome mat by the entrance caused a bell to go off when Apple walked in. Amused, he stepped on the mat several times, until at last he stood quietly in the center of the room, the smell of incense burning on an altar. That is when he heard weeping.

Her name was Mary the Fortune-teller and she was going through the saddest day of her life. Unfortunately for Mary, she was in love and had no premonition of what her lover had in store. In fact, she was not a mystic at all; she had developed a certain intuition and good common sense for her stock in trade, but none of that helped her now. In truth, she was blinded by passion. Her jealousy had grown to extremes and had brought her boyfriend to the edge of suffocation. In the end, she brought on herself the very fate she feared: he'd found a younger, less possessive girl and left her with a broken heart.

Mary woke up late, just as she always did, and went to the kitchen to grab a coffee. She usually opened the shop in the afternoon, so she figured she had time to relax before she became a mystic for hire. She didn't notice the silence at first; then she remembered that this was her boyfriend's day off. Next she discovered the closet was empty—along with everything in her wallet. She felt helpless so she went back to bed and cried hoping for a better day. That is when she heard the "Bing" of the welcome mat. She did not recall opening for business so she rushed through the beaded curtains and spied the stranger taking deep breaths.

"We're closing now and I'm on my way out," she told him.

"Are you the fortune-teller?" he asked.

"Yes," she said without looking. "It's time for my break and I need to get to the store. Come back later tonight!"

"I like your sign. It's true. I think everyone is unique—"

"You bet," Mary interrupted, grabbing her purse to guard what little she had left. "Listen, if this is a robbery, you're out of luck. I already got taken this morning." She stopped to give him a quick once-over. The stranger was rather attractive, young, and not at all unpleasant. Had she been in a better mood, she surely would have done a little flirting; but seeing as this was the worst day of her life, and romance the source of her burdens, Mary decided to best leave things be.

"You better go now," she told him, grabbing her keys.

"I am sorry." The stranger graciously bowed, and headed straight to the door, where he couldn't resist stepping on and off the mat.

"Ding dong, ding dong! Another incredibly wonderful dream!"

"Incredibly wonderful?" Mary laughed, and finally met his eyes. She was instantly intrigued, and felt as though she knew him well.

"Are you all right? I heard you weeping."

"I'm fine … thank you. Just a bad day."

"Do you know if the church is nearby? It's a building that's home to the pigeons. I need to talk to a preacher."

"It's only a few more blocks ahead. You can't miss it."

As the stranger stepped outside, Mary felt the urge to stop him. Maybe I should ask for his name, she wondered, or better yet, his number.

"I'll tell you what … I was going to get a lottery ticket so I'll walk up to the corner with you," she said. The stranger waited outside while she locked the bolts on the door.

"Isn't it an odd time for Church?" Mary asked as the two of them walked together.

"I was told that if I want to find out who dreams us, I had better talk to a preacher."

"That's so sweet." She smiled. "How come you're so sure that someone is dreaming us?"

"Don't you dream things?"

"Things like what?"

"The dreams you see when you're awake. Have you made any of them come true?"

"I'm working on it …" She sighed. "But I'm not having any luck!"

"Maybe you're not dreaming the right thing."

"What do you mean by that?"

"You must be careful about deciding who you are. It's easy to get the wrong idea—then you dream the wrong thing! At first I thought I could be a mechanic, then some sort of fixer, but I'm still not sure …"

"Those are incredibly wonderful things."

"Do you know a lot about human beings?"

70

"Not enough," Mary confessed. "I thought I knew my boy-friend but he took off this morning with all my cash. I should have known—I'm a fortune-teller ..."

"Can you tell me my fortune?" the young man eagerly asked.

Is this a trap? Mary started to wonder. Perhaps he's one of those city inspectors—or maybe a scam artist himself?

"It's an entire process," she answered carefully.

"Everything seems to be ..."

Mary could no longer keep up a front—this man already saw deep into her eyes. What he glimpsed, though, puzzled him. Here was the shadow of a dream, an empty space where the spark used to be. Mary's teary eyes were drying but their sadness stained her expression.

"What happened to your dreams?" he whispered; "where did all your dreaming go?" His question brought fresh tears.

"How could you say that to me?" she wept. "I have dreams! You saw something in my eyes! What is it?" Mary demanded.

"... Nothing," said the stranger, after a pause.

"Nothing?" Mary looked aghast.

"I see a place for it but it's not there. I can't find it ... Nothing is there."

"A place for what?" she desperately asked.

"The spark in the eyes of human beings. It's always there"—the man took a second look—"but in you ... well ... you have a space for it."

"Do you know how it feels to have a broken heart—to love someone so, that they can step all over you?"

Apple could feel her agony, passionate, intense, and filled with courage. How could someone with no spark in her eye show such signs? It was a mystery.

"Someone has broken your heart and now you have no spark in your eye"—he put it together like a mechanical diagnostic—"but why?"

"Because I love him. He took a piece of me, and that is the piece you see missing."

"I believe we are incomplete without each other because we're all part of one dream," Apple told her.

"That is so true ... Have you ever been in love?"

"I've been on a train; I rode in a patrol car; I fixed an engine ... I've also been to a beautiful beach, then to a gas station where a—"

"But you've never been in love, have you?" Mary repeated.

"Well ... I don't know; I could have been. Tell me more about it."

Mary thought on it awhile. "When you are in love with someone, nothing else matters. You care just about that person; you're safe, you're free, you're—"

"Not afraid?"

"Yes, you could say that."

"So you don't need safety glass?"

"What safety glass?"

"The safety glass people choose to live behind so they can be safe from others." The young man paused to consider. "Tell me, do people share it when they are in love, or do they get rid of it altogether?"

Mary never before thought of her love life that way. The stranger's words were provoking.

"That's interesting," she told him, charmed by the idea. "I have to think more about it ..."

"So being in love with another human being," he continued with the thought, "... is it like being one with the Great Feeling?"

"That's a beautiful way to put it ... You are one with another person. Two become one."

"But what about the rest of us—me and them, and everything else?" He pointed at passing pedestrians. "We are all part of one dream as well. Maybe you suffer because you choose to love only one human being."

"When you think you've found your other half, it's difficult to let go. Even if they just ripped you off."

"Your other half? Is that what you're missing?" He envisioned half a human being. "How could you be missing half of yourself when all of you is here?"

Mary looked him square in the eye. "You've never had a girlfriend, have you?"

"I met Daisy and Theresa but they weren't my other half." He then began to ponder. "Do you think I'm missing half of myself and that's why I don't know who I am?"

"Who are you?"

"Apple," he told her.

"You're all there, Apple," Mary assured him. "You know what? I will tell you your fortune. You're an easy one. You're going to find out who you are, and you're going to like it. If I've ever told anyone the right fortune, this is it."

"That's nice to hear—and don't worry, there's still a place for your other half." Apple checked in her eyes. "I can see it."

"Do you really?" Mary looked afraid. Had she truly come face to face with a mystic? Was this the price for her years of farce—to face the dire truth?

"What should I do?" she implored him. "I feel so empty without ..."

"Perhaps you can fill the space with your dreams."

"My only dream is to love somebody ... not everyone is so lucky, I guess."

"That's what Carlos told me. My friend was blind but dreamed of light so hard that now he can see. He told me not everyone is lucky enough to make their dream come true; yet I've found that everyone has a dream, even if they hide it far away. If yours is to find a human being to love, you can make it come true and fill the space in your eyes."

Mary was dumbstruck; speechless. Apple spoke with a wisdom that no self-styled seer could ignore. She felt cheap and dishonest, fake—but most of all, sorry for having ever toyed with people's emotions. The brokenhearted, the sad, the lonely, the desperate, the foolish: all had been through her shop, all had been lied to for the sake of a buck. Maybe that is why she hadn't any money—she didn't deserve it.

"Why is it that people turn away from each other when all they really want is each other?"

Apple stopped to consider the question. After several moments, he spoke. "A man who made his dreams come true told me that people often don't have the wherewithal to care for someone else—they are trapped, he said, inside their own worlds, mindful only of their interests. He said the streets are filled with dreamers, but they're afraid of one another. Is it true?"

"Yes," Mary responded.

"What about you—why aren't you dreaming? You have the space reserved for it."

"I-I don't know," she stammered; Apple's question caught her off guard.

"I believe you can dream your broken heart back."

Mary glared at him, defiant. "The love between a man and a woman cannot be compared to anything! True love is the most wonderful feeling there is!"

"But only you can fill the space in your eyes."

Mary lowered her head and stared at the sidewalk. Now the city was quiet, and the rain made the concrete glow. She thought of her boyfriend and how he had showed her less compassion than the stranger beside her. She heard tropical music from the corner store a few feet away, happy and passionate, celebrating life with every note.

"My name is Mary," she said at last. In that moment she felt comfortable and realized that a gorgeous male specimen now stood before her. The young stranger was beautiful and strong; his eyes shone with childlike purity—yet something behind his expression spoke with the knowledge of millennia. Perhaps he was the answer to her prayers, and she wondered if the incense had finally brought in good spirits.

Incredibly wonderful things … Mary started thinking, and remarkably, she began to believe in them—like falling in love all over again.

"Why did you come into my shop?" she asked.

"Because you're a fortune-teller. I thought you could tell me who I am."

"You really don't know?"

"Like everybody else, I want to become someone; so first I need to find out who I am."

"Nonsense," Mary replied. "Look at yourself—you're beautiful! Drop that silly idea of becoming someone! You read what my sign said, right? You are a miracle, you are unique, that's the way it goes. We're already a masterpiece—all of us."

"How do you find out what kind of masterpiece you are?"

"It'll come to you," she said. "Or you'll come to it ..." As she spoke these words, a vision came without warning—with the impetuousness of fire. The safety glass, she thought as she stared at him; we are so afraid. Then Mary understood how love could set her free. She leaned forward and gave Apple a kiss.

"You are my angel," she spoke softly.

Apple felt a jolt—he could not recall ever being kissed before; he felt electrified.

"You filled the space," Apple whispered to Mary, looking into the spark that glowed in her eyes. "I'm glad ... you could fix your broken heart ..."

Mary drifted into the market that day on a cloud; even the clerk couldn't help but notice her elation. "Give me a lottery ticket—I feel lucky tonight!" She laughed and turned to look outside. Yet Apple had already gone.

XII
The Dream Detector

The church was old and gray and hard to miss, just as the crows had said. A single spire topped with a cross stood against the sky; below it, long stairs led to three enormous doors. Across from the church was a parking lot, and beside it a school that occupied the entire block.

When Apple arrived at the complex, he was still thinking about Mary and her kiss. In the two minutes it had taken to walk three blocks, he had already asked himself if he was in love. He found the tingling intoxicating and impossible to resist, and it brought excitement that defied reason. He was gripped by an urge to return to her; but Apple overcame the moment and reminded himself of the task at hand: to find out more about the Dreamer.

It was the kiss, he concluded. That was the crucial moment—but once he overcame that weakening sensation, the feeling became more interesting. Apple felt lighter with every step, and joy overtook him. He thought of Mary's words, those that had brought the spark to her eye—"Drop that silly idea of becoming someone!" Her words rang true, the kiss yet vivid; in love, he felt like a masterpiece.

"It'll come to you," Mary had said, "or you'll come to it ..." Apple started to wonder if both had happened at once. Maybe he needed to understand that they helped make each other's dream come true.

"No wonder human beings fall in love," Apple murmured; the idea of sharing a piece of himself with another opened the world. This is why Mary could walk away by herself and not be alone; and why he could make it this far without returning in fear of losing that feeling. Perhaps, Apple thought, love is beyond a man and a woman, beyond the overwhelming kiss—the invisible engine at the root of all things, maybe the Great Feeling itself! Just then, he heard strange sounds.

"*Cooo roo, Coo roo,*" it called, passionate.

"*C'too coo,*" came the call from the tower, clearly some sort of love song. Apple looked up and there he saw, strutting along the edge, the source of the serenade.

Leonardo (as he was called by the resident preacher), an impressive orange-eyed fellow, ruffled his red and white plumage. Here was no ordinary pigeon; Leonardo was the greatest lover in the flock. That night he was romancing as usual, and his song could be heard for blocks. Apple stood on the steps enthralled.

"What a magical feeling connects all things!" he said aloud, startling the tender object of affection, who flew away into the shadows of the bell tower.

Leonardo glared at the intruder and, letting out his toughest sounding "*Oooorkkk!*," violently flapped his wings. Apple was particularly embarrassed.

"I'm terribly sorry I interrupted your song!"

The great lover came further out on the ledge and hopped down onto street level. He puffed his chest and bobbed his head up and down, bopping several times around Apple.

"I only recently experienced the feeling myself," Apple confessed to the bird, "and wasn't aware how many beings try to become one in pairs."

Leonardo could not believe his pigeon ears. He could actually understand human babble! This had to be some sort of magic. He knew about such tricks because his grandfather had flown out of a magician's hat a thousand times, until the day he decided to make a life on his own in the top of this bell tower.

"Where did you learn to talk pigeon?" a nervously pacing Leonardo asked.

"The crows say because I'm one with the Great Feeling ... they're the ones who sent me here."

"The crows?" Leonardo quickened his pace. "Did they happen to mention us?"

"Crows are not as bad as they seem," Apple responded. "You have to get to know them."

"What are they good for? Bullies!" Leonardo puffed up his chest in disgust. "Look how they go after sparrows! Claim to be mystical, in touch with the Spirit and all that mumbo jumbo! But what do crows know about, apart from hustling? We pigeons are lovers! And my friend, the night is young. So what are you looking for? I'm busy."

"I'm looking for a preacher. I was told I would find one here."

"Try during the day — and be sure to bring something to eat," Leonardo urged. "People don't come around at night. Preacher shuts the doors."

Apple looked up at the rest of the flock sleeping in the tower. "So why aren't you sleeping along with the others? Is it because of your song?"

"There are one hundred eleven in our flock," Leonardo bragged, "and one third of them are my offspring. I'm the world's greatest lover!"

"I can tell. It must all be part of the dream." Apple regarded him closely. "So whoever dreams me is also dreaming you. Your love song and dance—do you believe it comes from the Spirit?"

Leonardo came to a stop. He stretched up his neck and focused all his senses on the peculiar intruder. The aroma of blossoms was delicious, the whole aspect of him embracing; he had never met a human he could understand, but this one needed no words; he was pure feeling.

"What do you want preacher for?"

"I want to find out who I am, so I wish to talk to the preacher about the Dreamer."

"I know who you are—you're a lover, too!"

"I am," Apple affirmed. Dreaming awake and love are somehow connected—Apple sensed he was close to discovering how.

"This passionate attraction brought on by a kiss is what gives everyone a taste of the Dreamer—it gives humans the faith to have courage! To love is the choice," Apple reasoned aloud. How strange, then, that when it comes to love, people appear to have no choice at all.

"What a predicament!" Apple observed. "Yet people, whether alone or not, continue to dream when they're awake ..." Leonardo listened with his head half cocked. "But if love is needed to have faith, how can only one human feel it without another being? Where would love come from? Who would be the other half?"

Apple suspected love's mysteries encompassed much more than he knew.

"If you still wish to talk to preacher," Leonardo informed him, "I saw him over by the birch tree out back, going somewhere far underground, I think ... but it's going to take him a while. Love plenty!" With that, Leonardo flew to the top of the tower where his love dance began once more.

"*Cooo roo Cooo roo*" echoed across the church and reached the reverend's ears.

"Leonardo is at it again." Reverend Francis chuckled as he wiped the sweat off his forehead and dusted the dirt off his pants. He had been in that hole so long his eyelids felt heavy and the dirt felt soft and welcoming. But there was no time to waste, he had to continue.

Clunk ... clunk ... He shoveled more pounds of dirt into a bucket and looked up from the hole he'd been digging for the past several weeks. The sky was clear and the full moon shined along the sides of the hole, now a full fourteen feet deep. Francis wiped his glasses and admired the beauty of the scene. Maybe this is the night. Perhaps that evening the hole was illuminated for a good reason. He leaned against the ladder in the pit, and putting the shovel aside, lit another cigarette.

"Preacher with Penchant for Gambling Slips Out of Bankrupt Parish," he joked, but his was gallows humor. Francis could already see the press reports. Sooner or later the truth would come out. He would have to flee or face the judge. He took a nervous drag from his cigarette and continued to shovel the dirt—which continued to fall in around him. His face took on a miner's cast; shame mixed with desperation the deeper into the hole he dug. The air in the pit was moist and cold.

This hole reminded him of the grave, but the stakes outside were higher.   What will happen when the parishioners find out? Even after I'm gone there will be no escape. Francis had not yet taken off but already he carried the burden. He prayed that the Lord would have mercy and that he would be given a chance to rectify his mistake.

"The way you play the odds. The way you talk to God ... it all makes a difference," he repeated to himself as he reached for the metal detector.

About six months had passed since Francis started gambling again. It happened on a Saturday afternoon when he was invited to a fund-raising bingo. He had won so much money for the church that day he felt he was getting his old touch back. Within weeks, he was gambling on his own, buying lottery tickets and betting on anything from horses to football teams.

At first, things were going well. One win led to the next, and soon the good reverend had saved enough to buy himself that brand-new entertainment system he had always wanted; instead, he gambled it all away on a hockey game in hopes of buying a condominium. In fact, Francis felt so lucky on that unlucky afternoon that he grabbed all the church's funds from the bank and rang up his bookie with dreams of rebuilding the entire church complex.

Three hours later, the reverend had only debts and a pile of trouble. He went without food or sleep for two days until he could no longer pray.

The sign said $9.99. Francis stood outside the thrift store gazing in through the window.

"Good morning, Reverend," said the owner with a selling smile. "See anything you like?"

"Is that a metal detector?" Francis asked.

"A great buy!" said the salesman. "Works pretty well, too. It's great for the beach, if you're looking for treasure!"

Treasure was precisely what the Reverend needed: it was written all over his face—but the idea was too far-fetched.

"I'll give you a discount," said the man. Then he offered a demonstration by pointing the now beeping metal detector at a pipe nearby, insisting the reverend accept it as a donation to the church.

It was said that during the days of Prohibition the local preacher, who was a whiskey lover, had a deal with the bootleggers: they could use the church cellar for storage in exchange for gold. According to legend, the preacher got word of a raid and buried the gold somewhere on the church grounds but had no time to retrieve it before he fled.

The urgent beeping of the metal detector at first had come as a sign, a chance at redemption. He would take the money, pay back the church, and have plenty left for a full renovation. Digging this hole was merely his work for having to get out of one. Yet fourteen feet and three days later, the hole felt more like a grave than a promise. The reverend grabbed his metal detector and swung it in front of him one more time.

Beep, beep, beep … Apple could hear the loud sound buzzing through the night. He made his way around a parking lot and through an open gate that led into the vegetable garden. There were also several fruit trees, and a lovely carved wooden bench.

"Someone dreamed of this being here, too," Apple said into the night, "just like the one at the beach."

Beep, beep, beep … He followed the sound until he arrived at the back of the garden, where several buckets and a mountain of dirt sat next to a very deep hole.

Francis was furiously sweeping the instrument back and forth in the pit when he was startled by Apple's shadow. The stranger stood at the edge of the hole and peered down.

"What are you doing there?" Apple called to him, intrigued.

The man seemed surprised, as if caught doing something amiss. "This is private property," he said, quickly taking up his shovel. "What are you doing here?"

"Are you the preacher?"

"How can I help you?" Francis thought perhaps this could be an emergency.

"What can you tell me about the Dreamer?"

"I have no time for jokers." Here, surely, was another twisted mind better off in the hands of a doctor and he was in no mood for late-night counseling. He still had plenty of digging to do. So he put his detector aside and rolled down his sleeves to face the stranger.

"Are you an infidel?" he quietly demanded, "or a heretic?"

"I believe I'm a lover," Apple responded.

"Are you looking for trouble?" Francis came up the ladder. "I'm afraid I am going to ask you to leave."

"What is down there?" Apple contemplated the depth of the hole.

"I don't know … " Francis brushed the dirt off his clothes. "Something."

"My friend told me preachers love to talk," Apple began.

"Is there something you need to talk about?"

"I'm trying to find the Dreamer. The one who dreams us," Apple explained. "I want to know who I am, and I believe the way to find out is to meet the dreamer who dreamed me."

"Have you opened your heart to the Lord?"

"Who is that? I don't believe we've ever met," responded Apple.

"What's your faith, son?" Francis asked warily.

"I don't know … what do you think?"

"What do you believe in?" Francis rephrased the question.

"I believe in dreams. I saw how it brought someone back to her feet, and how another dreamed his sight back! Yet something nurtures it all … Have you ever been in love? It makes you believe!"

"Do you have a religion?" Francis clarified one more time.

"Am I supposed to have one? I don't have a suitcase either. George thought I should have one. What is a religion?"

"How could you not know? Everyone has a belief."

"Human beings believe many things," Apple reflected. "Are there many religions?"

"Yes," Francis responded, "but we have the truth. The Lord gives us a choice to embrace Him or not."

"People have a choice to dream what they wish," Apple concurred. "So who dreams all the religions?"

The reverend was appalled. "You try to understand too much when all you have to do is believe," he explained. "Let the Lord into you heart and you shall understand everything."

"That makes sense … to understand everything means to know the Dreamer because he is dreaming everything!"

"Outrageous!" the reverend cried. He had never heard such nonsense. "The Lord is not a dream, nor is He a dreamer!"

Apple noticed fire kindling in the preacher's eyes; though he appeared angry, his expression was empowered by a faith all consuming, all loving. He understood then that this man loved greatly beyond himself, a love that did not need a kiss to ignite. Here was a revelation: an all-embracing love, the stuff of dreams.

"We are unique. I am sure he loves us all, and all of us love him … but maybe everyone dreams him differently," Apple said after a pause. "It is the way of human beings, the way we are dreamed. Everyone I've met had a dream, but you are dreaming the dream itself."

All at once the nonsense stopped and Apple's gibberish started to make perfect sense. Francis saw the purity in his heart. He perceived no arrogance, nor assumption behind the young man's words; they came from a place so sincere and well intended that the reverend felt rather ashamed.

"Be not deceived. God is not mocked: for whatsoever a man soweth, that shall he also reap—Galatians six-seven A," Francis quoted. "I am not what I seem. Why do you think I am digging this hole? I do have a dream," he confessed.

"And is it buried inside that hole somewhere?"

"This hole is my temptation," the reverend avowed, "for the love of money is the root of all evil: which while some have coveted after, they have pierced themselves through with many sorrows—Timothy six-ten."

Apple looked confused. "Why are you speaking names and numbers?"

"They are from the Bible. The book where all is written! But I'm afraid my love for money may not deem me worthy of it."

"People love money?" Apple sounded genuinely surprised.

What sort of man is this who does not know the lure for gold? the reverend pondered. The scent of apples infused the air and Francis felt exposed.

"I went astray," he confessed to the stranger. "Now all I pray for is another chance."

"So what's in the hole?" Apple seemed interested. His tone was unobtrusive, comfortable and understanding; it made Francis open his heart.

"Redemption," he whispered.

"How long have you been digging?"

"I got the metal detector a few days ago and it started beeping on this spot. I began to dig and found gold dust in the dirt … I only intended to go down three or four feet, but the deeper I dug, the louder the beeps—so loud you can hear it a block away. Now I'm afraid to use it." Francis got down on his knees to reach for the ladder. He was ready to climb back down into the hole to lay hold of the metal detector when the ground shook violently beneath them. The walls of the hole collapsed on themselves and within seconds, the treasure-finding gizmo was buried under twelve feet of dirt.

Beeep, beeep, beeep … the muffled sound could be heard coming out of the ground into the quiet night. Francis was stunned, his heartbeats were wild: had he been in that hole, he would be buried as well.

Apple stood calmly and listened, feeling the vibration under his feet when the beeping grew fainter, then stopped.

"Maybe it was a dream detector," he said to Francis, who sat, badly shaken, on the dirt. "Perhaps it stopped because you've found what you're looking for."

"My life's been spared," he told Apple, giving him a warm, grateful hug. For the first time in many years he truly felt blessed. "You've ended my nightmare!" Francis cried out; he had found redemption and forgiveness.

"I've committed a terrible crime," he confessed. "I gambled the church's funds away. I had a winning streak, you see, and I just fell back into it. I thought I would never do that again." Francis shook his head and laughed at the moon. Apple understood the reverend had something to say and listened carefully.

"That's why I was digging—see?" The preacher showed Apple what used to be the pit. "I was looking for the treasure so I could put the money back, and then some! Ridiculous, no? But that is all I want. Forgiveness is divine, my friend; that is why I was spared the grave I dug for myself."

Apple and the preacher contemplated the moonlit crater before them. During that moment of serenity, Francis put himself in the hands of the Lord and promised he would confess his crime and tender his resignation. Apple could see the dream in his eyes, made of courage, passion, and incommensurable faith; not the usual spark he had witnessed before. It was a lighthouse, a calling, a star guiding the way.

"The Dreamer gives everyone a choice of dreaming him," he quietly told the reverend. Francis smiled and glanced at the moon while searching for his cigarettes, but he realized they were buried in the ground with the rest of his weaknesses.

"I think I'll quit smoking as well," he said.

A love song broke through the silence and Francis flashed a fatherly smile.

"That's Leonardo!" he told Apple. "The Great Lover! Did you know pigeons can fly fifty miles per hour? Follow me ..." and the reverend walked back to the front of the church to take a better look at the tower. "Pigeons also have strong homing instincts that help them find their way back from great distances."

Apple looked into the preacher's eyes. All the pain and anguish was gone. Yet what truly happened? Did the reverend find his dream in that hole? Or had he actually found the Dreamer?

Feel your way, Apple recalled Leonardo's advice, your destination will bring you to it. He reminded himself that although he was no pigeon, he certainly was a lover—and love was taking him somewhere. The path was effortless, the calling clear: all one had to do was to feel it. Apple rejoiced, and in that moment of great understanding he remembered his friend the crab.

"How wise was his advice! Learn more about human beings!" The animals spoke the language of the dreamer, the Great Feeling spoke through them! "And how right are the pigeons too!" He had been heading home all along.

There was no need to search for what was everywhere; the Dreamer had been talking to him from the moment he woke up at the apple orchard. But searching was not his destination; it had been his point of departure. Something "incredibly wonderful" lived in the hearts of human beings, something so exceptional not even the Dreamer could be without; Apple understood what he had to do. He smiled and his expression was so delightful the reverend realized Apple believed in something he had stopped believing in a long time ago.

"People don't believe in people anymore," he said to Apple. "You have a gift. You made me see that."

The priest woke up early and that morning at service, he stood on the podium in front of an expecting audience; it was not the usual sermon. He did not preach of doom, Armageddon, or redemption, nor heaven or hell, he did non mentioned, heretics or infidels, instead of crying outrage for the armies of the Lord, or pointing fingers at the sinners, he opened his holy book and began with these words:

"If a man say. I love God, and hateth his brother, he is a liar: for he that loveth not his brother whom he hath seen, cannot love God whom he hath not;" and that became the word that day, and it belonged to everyone.

Will they understand stealing? Addiction? Weakness? Francis begged The Lord to allow him to continue His Work for that was the one thing in the world he loved the most. He stood silently amongst the cheers, ready to confess his crime to the parish when a woman named Mary approached him with a generous donation to renovate the church. She claimed she had won the lottery after she had dreamed the number, but Francis knew otherwise.

From that day on, the church opened its doors to all, and Francis would often tell a tall tale about a pigeon named Leonardo and a dream detector.

"See that apple tree in the garden! Well, that was a hole once," the story would always begin with those words.

XIII
The End of the Fight

When Apple left the church grounds, he had but one thing in his mind: to meet more people. Even when they can't make their dreams come true, people still need something to believe in, he thought; belief is the force behind dreams, the key to knowing who you are. That feeling gives us a choice to make our own dream, Apple believed, and its secret lay like buried treasure deep in the human spirit. The Dreamer is everywhere, he thought; and Apple was in love with the dream.

As he strolled down the city streets, Apple couldn't help but to notice the people. They were everywhere, walking in out of buildings, inside cars, eating behind restaurant windows. They were laughing, thinking, charging ahead, and daydreaming from balconies. How strange, he thought, that people believe in things they can't see but have a hard time believing in each other. Yet he could see the glow in their eyes; on the street, behind windshields, inside the stores. One heart. Infinite voices. Apple was enchanted. This was his way home.

"People don't believe in people," he said aloud, "but why?" He had to find out.

BrrrrrrMMMM! the sound of a powerful engine roared behind him followed by an earsplitting screech. The acrid stench of burning rubber pierced the air and a cloud of smoke swirled above the asphalt. Apple turned around in excitement—*What sort of machine is this? Surely a wonderful dream!* What he saw was not a dream but rather a nightmare: a black-and-yellow sports car with fat wheels and fancy rims flying through the air like a rogue rocket, its shiny chrome grille twirling a set of angry teeth. The car had turned the corner at tremendous speed, too fast for the grip of its racing tires. The massive yellow chunk of metal flipped in the air, rolling twice down the street before it smashed against a tree.

Everything happened in a split second. Apple was the only witness. He stood silently and looked around. He had walked for so long and in such deep thought that he had no idea where he was. The area looked industrial, for the most part storage and factories, and the scant few stores were closed. He noticed a park nearby. The streets were deserted.

The roar of a second car broke the silence, as loud and ripping as the first. A large blue vehicle with tinted windows appeared from around the corner. It slowed down to check on the accident while its driver revved the engine. The yellow car was crushed and a curtain of smoke started billowing out of it. The windows in the blue car slid down slowly and two young men in shades peeked from inside. Apple couldn't see their eyes but he could feel hate peering out from behind their glasses. After a few seconds of examining the smoking car, they pulled out their guns and fired into it without so much as flinching.

Pop-p-pop-pop pop! ...

Apple froze under the safety of shadows and watched the aggressors empty their pistols from across the street. The thunder snapped for several seconds. He recoiled at the barrels spitting flames and the stinging smell of burnt gunpowder. "Somebody dreamed that too!" he cried. The vision reminded him of Ruphus and his warnings, of George and his loneliness, of Luke and his prison—but most of all, it gave new meaning to the preacher's words, that "people don't believe in people anymore." This was all too much for Apple to accept—who felt such sorrow for the world that he never stopped to think how lucky he was that the thugs had not yet noticed him. He felt a profound, tremendous sadness.

The killers slid their windows back up and vanished into the night as fast as they had appeared. Less than thirty seconds to Apple seemed an eternity. In a mere moment, a quiet street had turned into an inferno and a horrific feeling hung in the air where the blue car had been. There were no pedestrians to ask for help or passing cars to stop; Apple was alone with the disaster.

"Am I dying? This cannot be," the driver asked himself inside the crashed vehicle. He could feel the heat of the burning engine scolding his feet. A treacherous smoke engulfed him and his eyelids felt heavy.

"I will not give up," he whispered.

Apple ran toward the vehicle but before he could reach it he saw a figure crawling out of the smoke—a young man, about his age. He had no hair and his head was bleeding. When he saw Apple approaching, he scrambled to his feet and ran from the car.

"Get away! It's going to blow!" he screamed just as the vehicle exploded. The man threw himself to the ground and landed at Apple's feet. Pieces of metal shot in the air and the car became a stack of thick smoke.

"You're hurt," Apple told him, "you must wait for the truck with the lights."

"I've gotta get out here!" The young man quaked, leaping back to his feet. Apple looked into his eyes: a maddening fire burned in them. He was terrified.

"Who were those men?" Apple asked.

Sirens broke in above the fearsome crackling of the burning wreck. The young man put his hand to his head and covered the open wound. The blood continued to flow down his forehead, making it difficult for him to see, but he kept looking around as though still being chased, then took off down the street.

"Wait!" Apple said, running after him. "Where are you going?

The young man ran and ran, hopping across streets and alleys until he finally made it to a park several blocks away. He clawed through the bushes like a wounded animal, staying in the shadows until he reached the top of a hill; here he could view the scene below. Dozens of ambulances, fire trucks, and police cars illuminated a column of multicolored smoke that wafted into the sky. He was surrounded.

For this young man of twenty-five, the world had become an obstacle; but David was still full of dreams. He carried the old neighborhood in his heart and embodied it with every move and expression that came out of his mouth—but he could not understand why the world didn't see that there was a lot more to him beyond that. He tried to understand, to live in the world, but all the world wanted was for him to stay in his.

They could not see his dreams, or his mother's, or even the dreams of his neighbors; they did not know what his prayers were for, or what a sixteen-hour shift felt like. What was suffering good for, if there was no pardon? Frustration built, resentment mounted, and soon enough, David became like a flaming sword that would burn and slice through anyone; and so he came to be.

"The David Show" had started late one night two years earlier, then quickly became an upheaval. It began with David hiding in a corner of a room, turning on a tape recorder and beginning his rant; all his rage spilled out like bitter poison. Night after night, the tapes piled up.

Racial injustice, poverty, equality, human rights, government corruption; David had an opinion about everything that mattered. His views rang true for many—unfortunately for him. His friends shared his recordings and posted them on the Web, where he soon became a celebrity. Before too long, a local AM station offered him a late-night slot, and David hit the airwaves. The Mouth, as they called him, was a nocturnal menace, attacking issues that affected his community one by one. News articles and TV interviews followed, and soon The Mouth became a dangerous man.

In the three weeks since David's crusade against violence, his efforts started to show results. He began to expose the neighborhood gangs, not by name, but by description; and he was urging their families—not to mention local authorities—into taking action. The gangs had a better idea.

"Good-bye baby!" David cried from the bushes atop the hill. "I loved that car, he said as sirens wailed from all directions and a helicopter could be seen approaching. Spotlights trained on the smoke that drifted from the wreck.

"Why did you come here?" whispered a voice from the darkness.

"Who's there?" David gasped, sliding back into the bushes.

"It's me," Apple said, "I followed you here."

David took a peek. He recognized the stranger from the crash site, eyes full of concern.

"It's beautiful."

"What?"

"The spot where we stand. It's pretty."

"Uh huh … last pretty spot 'roun here," David said, distracted by all the sirens. "They're turnin' it into a mall." A whiff of burning gasoline brought on a sense of fear; David was quaking in the brush.

"Once the cops see there's no one in the car, word will get out fast and they'll start lookin'," he whispered. "If they take me, I'll be dead before I hit the hospital. The guys you asked me about—the ones with the guns—they have friends and I don't know those cops down there. You better get out before they see you."

"Who are they?"

"Bad people."

"With bad dreams."

"Yeah, that's right, with very bad dreams," David assured him. "How many of them were there?"

"The windows in front did not go down. Two were in the back."

"I know who they are. They won't get away with this."

"Do you think they have any good dreams too?"

David stopped to think. His head wound oozed a bit, but the bleeding had calmed. "Maybe," he said, surprised by his words. At any other time the question would have provoked a flat-out no, but the way it was asked made him circumspect.

"How long have you been running?"

"I'm hidin' from them. Not runnin'."

"Why?"

"Because I'm gonna fight them later."

"Do you think it's true people don't believe in people?"

"You should split," David suggested.

Apple thought a moment. "Seems to me that everyone can use someone to believe in … Have you ever been in love?"

"No," blurted David.

"Do you love something?"

"Yeah, I love a lot of things. I love my car, my mother, my

job, my skull ring, and the tattoo on my right shoulder—what do you want, man? Did they send you to kill me? Go ahead. Where is your gun? Or are you gonna cut me?"

"You're hurt because you love something. What do you believe in?"

"I believe enough to fight," David told him. "If you want justice, you gotta fight for it."

"Do you know anything about engines?"

"Matter of fact, I do. Why?"

"Think of a human being dreaming of one: every dream can be brought into this world. Good or bad, it appears to be a choice. It can be an engine or a gun."

"I don't need a gun. I have a microphone."

"And what do you do with it?"

David laughed. He didn't know where to begin. "I try to fix the world," he said.

"You love this world, don't you?"

David carefully considered the stranger.

"That must have been some engine in your car. It was loud."

"Vee-twelve engine. Eight hundred horsepower. Top speed, two hundred fifty-two miles an hour. That was my baby. Built her myself."

"You build engines!" Apple exclaimed with great excitement. "Wonderful! How do they work?"

"Well, the basics … there's fuel in it and it burns and it makes the pistons move and that's what makes the wheels turn ... You really should get outta here—"

"Just like a human being," Apple interrupted. "Do you know what fuels your dreams? Is it love or anger?"

"Listen, I been tryin' to get rid of a pack of murderers that are prowling the streets of my neighborhood. I'm talkin' scum here, guys who push dope on little kids and shoot people down in cold blood because they're on the wrong side of the street. Now they want to kill me. You decide whether it's love or anger. I don't really care."

Apple immediately thought of the preacher, who had dug himself into a hole too deep and was mad for it; the urban rebel was different: he could not see that his hole had collapsed on itself.

"My friend the Reverend was almost buried alive trying to look for redemption. In the end he found love, but first he had to dig a very deep hole ... And nothing really happened until the hole collapsed and his dream detector stopped."

"I ain't diggin' any holes," David snapped at the madness.

"But you," Apple explained, "you're hurt."

Hurt—the word rang so true it crawled under his skin and made him clench his fists in the shadows; all the pain came back, slicing his soul. The preconceptions, looks, and racial slurs burned inside him like a red hot coal. This was what The Mouth was made of: bitterness, frustration; but if these were his reasons, what were his dreams? David could barely remember. He smiled at the stranger and relaxed.

"I was an ambitious little kid. I wanted to be famous since I was four."

"Be somebody."

"Not somebody—I wanted to be Number One!" He gently touched the wound on his forehead. "But the world wouldn't let me. They would tell me what to do. Limit me. I don't like that. After a while I got desperate. More frustrated, difficult. I made more enemies than friends. Some days I couldn't even deal with myself, and you know why? All because of this dream you're talkin' bout, because every day it slipped further and further away ... until it became an illusion. I ain't big on denial, so when I see myself in a ditch I try to climb my way out. I'm gonna fight, know what I mean? So I fought and guess what? I won myself a war. The fightin' will never stop. It'll just keep on gettin' worse." David spoke with a devastating conviction.

"It must be difficult to fight against all things ... it's so easy to love them," Apple offered.

The Mouth was silenced by emotion. After a while, the stranger's words seemed to soothe and invigorate him. Fear and anger dissipated, his sense of loss replaced with inner stirring. David stood up from the bushes and felt his breath.

"I used to come up here a long time ago. This is where I made my plans to take over the world—back when I still loved everybody!" Never could he have imagined then that he would become a crusader. Yet his noble cause was not a happy one; it tainted his heart. Back when he was a kid, those were happier times. He could almost taste the ice cream and smell the roasting marshmallows on the beach. Good times.

"It's not true," he said at last. "People still believe in people."

"People believe in you, don't they?"

The sirens had quieted down and the helicopter left, but lights continued to flash all around the crash; for David, it was a spectacle worth witnessing. There, atop that hill, the playground of his youth, David understood how he had ended up a refugee in its shadows. Pain and fear had given him a cause strong enough to replace his dream and he had taken the bait. The demons that made him run had brought him back to this same hill where his dream had begun.

As David remembered, a smile took over his face. Thousands of letters, gifts, and hugs of gratitude flashed through his memory. The adoration and tears, the handshakes of respect; his path had been long and difficult, but things were changing, now even the gangs were afraid of him. David had become a dream himself. He spoke for those who had no voice, and people believed in him. Perhaps anger had turned him into what he was, and maybe he didn't like it as much as he thought he would, but at that moment he came to terms with it. He felt complete.

"My name is David," he said.

"Apple." Apple nodded. "Everyone is afraid. People hide from each other because they are afraid—of being rejected, misunderstood, not loved; of suffering. Yet that very thing brings sorrow. The path to the dream belongs to every one of us. Without that understanding, though, we're nothing but lonesome travelers. You've shown me treasure, something I couldn't understand."

"What treasure? What could I possibly show you?"

"I found that what makes a human unique is the ability to see dreams when awake," he explained. "Dreams are not easy to see, and even harder to realize."

David nodded.

"So a person must have passion and gather courage to truly believe in something," Apple continued. "But faith comes only from love, and love is harder to see than the dream."

"What does any of that have to do with me?"

"The dream is perfect, as is the world; imperfection is in our perception. You fought in anger, you got hurt and felt sorrow, but while you thought you had lost your dream, love was bringing you home. The only difference between you and those you fight is how far along the path you've come; you are all part of the journey."

"And where does this path lead to?"

"To you, me, and them. To one thing."

"Where are you from?" David asked, intrigued by his newfound advisor.

"I'm not sure," Apple told him, "I can't remember, nor do I recall my name. I must have been like everybody else, with a name and a dream I saw every day. Maybe I even made some of them come true! But I've learned things by just calling myself Apple."

"Apple," David smiled. The name rang to him with a sweetness worthy of its meaning. "Your name is new. What about your dream?"

"All I can see is the world, and you are in it, David. I cannot think of a better one."

The world, David thought. He had never heard a word more beautiful. He stepped back and looked at the scene of the accident: for the first time in years he feared nothing, he had nothing to fight.

"I'm ready to go home," David said, "where you headin'?"

"I'm already there."

"Take care of yourself. You really should see the doctor 'bout your memory loss."

"The doctor?" Apple asked, open to suggestions.

"Yeah," David told him, pointing through the park. "Bill! That's his name, yes," David exclaimed as if he had a revelation. "He's there now, at the hospital across the street. Maybe you should check it out. How long you plan to stay here?"

"Moment to moment," Apple smiled.

David laughed and hopped down the hill. Apple took the moment to feel the breeze against his skin and watched David disappear into the woods below.

"The world!" Apple repeated to himself. It was perfection beyond understanding. This is where questions stopped and Apple enjoyed the silence.

He walked slowly down the hill. Yes, Apple thought, the dream is perfect—but what a great burden without understanding! Admiring the swaying of leaves and the sounds of crickets, with every step he reflected on his day. He remembered the sign at the garage and understood the pain that brought Will's dad courage; he had visions of Theo, whose mistakes drowned him in sadness; of Mary trying to complete her other half; of Luke's prison of glass; and of the reverend's weakness. They all had dreams and choices that had to be made. What pain unleashed on the world—and so many obstacles, Apple thought. *Passion burning aimlessly, love misunderstood ...*

A new feeling overtook him. Apple was experiencing suffering. For all those dreaming behind glass, for those trying to fill the space, for the sad, lonely, and lost, and for all who fight, hide, or dig themselves into collapsing holes—for everyone who was or ever would be—Apple cried a tear, the first he could remember.

XIV
Dream Well

The lesson Apple had learned from his meeting with David had a profound effect. His identity did not seem so important. What difference did a name make? Is it not all the same dream, the same suffering?

He continued down the hill with these thoughts in mind, recalling the faces of those whom he had met, those sparks in all those eyes; and with every step he felt as though he were embracing each person all over again. Apple glimpsed their dreams: he saw Daisy's daughter in school, and Luke the train conductor proudly in his uniform; he felt the light in Carlos's eyes and heard the strum of Will's song. Suffering was not enough to extinguish their love. Then Apple was overtaken by a compassion so strong it rushed through him with invigorating power.

He ran and ran through the trees and grass, shining light on the world, like one of George's stars. His quest for understanding became a loving embrace and, immersed in gratitude, he contemplated his fate.

"How lucky to see," he said, recognizing that too many don't ever think of the dream, or do so only when it's too late. They would rather fight or hide or give up. It is difficult to love all things. Apple felt blessed. He danced and sang and leaped through the woods in joyful tribute to Leonardo the Lover, until at last he arrived at the gates of the park and stopped at the sight of a tree. Tall and round, the tree triggered thoughts of where everything had started earlier that day; Apple approached it slowly.

What hides so deeply within me that does not allow me to remember? Apple considered the tree. And does it really matter?

This tree was more than a familiar image, it felt like a very old friend. The feeling brought a smile whose origin he could not grasp, from a distant time when he must have known his name. How was it that he could embrace the universe, yet not remember why a tree made him smile? Perhaps struggle has to do with growth, like George's stars being born in the sky or blue crabs crossing the river against the tide. Suffering is as real as the world; it creates fear, its biggest lie— and like any lie, it is capable of causing incalculable misfortune.

"I am my only obstacle," Apple cried out and smiled at the city, "for when reality is in darkness, it is up to us to light the fuse in our heart; nothing else will light the way." For Apple, truth was the only memory worth keeping.

"Tell me tree," he asked loudly, "why do you make me smile?" His voice echoed across the park without a response. The city was sleeping and all he could hear was the never-ending song of crickets. He laughed. The tree made him smile because it was bursting with life. A human being, just like the tree, has to grow and bear fruit; it has to be nurtured with all that is good until it is ready for the world. Otherwise, the fruit will die and eventually so will the tree. It is the nature of the dream.

"What I was, I am not. Yet I was always who I am now." It was a declaration of feeling that came oddly, from behind his thoughts. "All I know is this love that binds me to you," Apple said to the tree, "and to the earth and the star and the air that blows your leaves. How is it that I find you, yet not myself?"

Apple looked around and sank into reminiscence, of love and suffering and the peace of compassion, but still he did not know who he was. Why was he holding on to these thoughts when what he needed to know was already his?

"I'm a human being," he said, "and this here is a tree... and we're alive!" Inhaling the fresh night air, Apple set his eyes on the street beyond the city park gates.

Bill left the emergency room at 4 A.M. and headed to the doctor's lounge. He grabbed a hot tea and sat on a couch, hoping to be left alone. Today was his birthday, but Bill wasn't the party type and he was careful not to let anyone know. Who needs to blow out candles in a hospital lounge in the early hours of the morning?

In a little while his shift would be over and he planned to

celebrate with eight hours of sleep. The night shift was a killer and he always tried to avoid it, but the hospital had an urgent need for experienced ER doctors; the director himself had asked him.

Bill—or Doctor Hajim, as his patients knew him—had always been a luminary. His parents were very religious, and his mother induced compassion and understanding in the boy from very early on. Billy always saw the world in a different light. He was a scientist, obsessed with the nature of things, from the tail of a wounded lizard to the hair on his father's arm. For him all life was filled with wonder; he was a natural-born researcher.

Yet something in particular made Billy unique: he dreamed things that belonged to other people. Often the dreams were messages for which he had no use, describing events he couldn't relate to and people whom he'd never met. The dreams were an intrusion. The boy was never able to make sense of them until the day Mr. Morris, who lived next door, got sick and was taken away by the ambulance.

That evening, old man Morris came to Billy in his dream and asked him to tell his wife that he was fine; moreover, he instructed the boy to look for a key inside a pocket in his old Air Force uniform that opened a box inside his desk. That same morning, little Billy ran to the house next door and gave Mrs. Morris the message. She burst into tears and ran over to the desk, where she found a box filled with stocks and bonds and many other valuables, including his will. Mr. Morris in fact had passed away the night before, so he needed the boy and his talents.

When Billy's mother found out about the miracle, she understood that her son was blessed with a gift. His father, however, was spooked by the idea, and he never accepted that his son could be psychic. He was afraid that others would see his son as a freak, so instead he blamed allergies and indigestion to account for his son's dreams. From that moment on, he forbade them to mention the subject in public.

Billy, though, kept on dreaming strange and prophetic things. The dreams turned into nightmares, more frequent and intense, and he became afraid to go to sleep. His nights were spent wide-eyed in bed until he passed out from exhaustion, only to dream another nightmare. He lost his appetite and grew ill.

"The dreams are messing around with his head!" he overheard his mother tell his father. "We've got to do something before it gets worse." Billy was concerned for their happiness.

So late that night, tucked in bed, he whispered to the dreams and told them that he was just a little boy, and that he had his own dreams to dream. He explained that the other people's dreams had to stop. He whispered for so long that his eyelids grew heavier and he succumbed to lack of sleep, to dream yet another dream.

He saw a tree, standing alone on a field. The sky glowed a tapestry of colors and a breeze swayed the graceful grass. He approached the tree in awe of its splendor and noticed lush red apples hanging from its boughs. He was about to grab one when a gentle voice spoke.

"Don't be afraid, Billy," it told him. *"Dream well."*

Billy opened his eyes that morning and immediately noticed a difference: he was not afraid. The strange dreams never came back after that and the years made their memory fade.

By the time Bill had graduated from the university, he'd consigned the entire experience to the realm of boyhood fantasy. He viewed his dreams as distortions caused by a form of psychosis brought on by deeply religious parents and a febrile imagination. Yet in spite of those explanations, Bill always kept that one dream in his heart—the dream that had stopped them all. He never understood it, but he'd spent years trying to interpret it in a hundred different ways. Ever since, he had decided to use his talents, shrouded as they were in mystery, to help people; that is why Bill became a doctor—that is how the dream had changed him.

Bill Hajid was still a young man. He was in his late thirties, divorced, no kids. For eight straight years he had been an ER surgeon, and in that time he'd seen an eternity of suffering. His heart had hardened, hope held little meaning; the fight against mortality was the only language he understood. Yet despite himself, on that lonely birthday, down and troubled, the doctor recalled the words from his last dream.

Don't be afraid, Billy … he found comfort in the words. "Dream well," he whispered, wishing he could believe in something again. The truth is that Bill felt like he could no longer help anybody. He was a lonely man who had ceased to see the beauty and joy in the world. He felt incomplete, as if a part of himself had gone away with the dreams. Doctor Hajid hid these feelings even from himself, but they sat with him in the lounge that night.

Doubt set in and he felt as if the whole of creation had gone into shadows. There was nothing to hope for, nothing to dream. Life was suffering. Bill felt himself slipping into the darkness. He sipped his tea and reflected on his last case. The patient had arrived in a coma less than an hour ago; he had suffered a severe blow to the head, had several broken ribs, and most of his body was burned. Bill worked hard trying to save him but in the end he lost him.

The phone started ringing within minutes of the man's arrival, and an hour later, dozens of people were crowding the lobby, moaning and crying until security had to move them outside. Bill walked out of surgery powerless and defeated. All his knowledge and skill had failed to revive the patient, and now a man people truly loved was dead. Had it been me on the table, Bill told himself, the hospital would still be searching for a relative.

He sat on the couch disenchanted. "Maybe all I need is someone to talk to," he said to the empty room. He finished his tea and stepped outside to the hospital garden, away from the buzz of the emergency room and headed straight toward a bench under a tree. No patients were on that side of the building and at those early hours only half the lights were kept on. The horizon hinted at dawn. He closed his tired eyes and in that lonely play of light and shadow Bill was puzzled by a sweet scent that filled the air.

Apple blossoms? he wondered; the hospital garden had never been so fragrant.

"Are you the doctor?"

He was startled by the voice of a stranger. "Yes," he said. "How can I help you?"

"I can't remember who I am," Apple explained. "I must have a name."

"Did you hit your head?"

"I don't remember," Apple told the doctor.

Bill pulled out a small flashlight from his coat pocket and pointed it at the stranger's pupils. "You seem to be fine ... any headaches or dizziness?"

"No."

"You need to get an X ray, and I would recommend an MRI. Have you checked in up front?"

"Checked in?"

"Who brought you here?"

"The dream, I suppose," Apple made clear to the doctor.

"... The dream?" Bill said, astonished.

"I came looking for you. A man named David told me you might be able to tell me who I am."

"Me? I'm an emergency room doctor. You need to see a specialist."

"But you're the physician here?"

"I am," Bill said, intrigued. The stranger's voice had a familiar ring that Bill hadn't failed to recognize.

"Who do you say recommended me?"

"David."

"David ... I don't know a David."

"Are you Bill?" Apple asked.

"That is my name. How far back can you remember?"

"Everything that's happened since I woke up this morning under the apple tree."

"The apple tree?" Bill froze. The mere mention of dreams and apple trees was enough to spook him—but the prairie scent in the air clinched it. He put his flashlight away and glanced up and down the garden. They were alone. He slipped his hands into his pockets and contemplated the situation. He'd seen temporary amnesia, but those cases typically involved physical trauma; the young man before him looked radiant. Bill thought someone might be playing a joke, but he quickly recalled he'd never told anyone about the dream or mentioned the apple tree. No, he considered, this is too far-fetched—he has to be telling the truth.

"A lapse in memory can be caused by many things," he informed the young man, "usually by some sort of trauma. It doesn't necessarily have to be physical, it can also be caused by emotional ... " he trailed off, stopping short. A kind of serenity in the young man's eyes silenced the physician. His was an awareness beyond words, a love he'd seen in the eyes of patients seconds before they died. Yet this young man seemed perfectly healthy. He was smiling, bright-eyed before him.

"Tell me more about the apple tree," the doctor asked, puzzled. "Where is it?"

"On a field, where a breeze blows the grass and the apples roll down a knoll."

Bill was shocked. "I know the place ... " he began, turning pale. The innocence of the young man's expression was a striking contrast to the wisdom in his eyes.

"Wonderful!" Apple exclaimed.

"Does it have a name?"

"Eden Orchards. That's what Slim calls it."

"Slim?"

"Yes. He used to be a salesman. The field is beyond the orchard, and if you walk from there, you'll find a marsh with blue crabs where Theo has a boat; and beyond that is a town where Will runs his father's garage and a road where Officer O'Reilly hides her patrol car behind a sign for Le Blue Crab Restaurant. She is a very good cop who loves to serve and protect; her first name is Theresa."

David, Slim, Theo, Will, Theresa, Le Blue Crab Restaurant—Bill had trouble keeping track. He liked how the stranger who smelled of blossoms talked about the world as if everyone knew one another.

Apple smiled at the beauty of it all, but especially at the bench. To him it was a temple of awareness, a symbol of human reflection.

"A park bench is a beautiful dream," he said. "People always put them in wonderful places. There's a bench on the beach where

Carlos got his sight. Why do you think people dream of park benches?"

"Because they're tired."

"Tired of what?"

Bill took a moment to think. "Of ugliness," he said.

"Great beauty is in this dream, and it hides within us. I believe everyone, deep inside, wishes to reveal it."

Bill was perplexed, speechless on the bench, while all his senses tingled. Here was a strange sensation to which he was no stranger; he remembered it very well.

"A long time ago, I had a dream about an apple tree—"

"And now you dream about it when you are awake," Apple reminded him.

Bill was a rational man, but the feeling was taking him back to a time when he believed in fantastic things. He couldn't lie to himself.

"Have you ever felt like you're going insane?" the doctor blurted aloud. He masked his fears with a wicked laugh.

Apple remained silent. He could feel the pain Bill carried inside, harsh and heavy, that drained all his strength. Bill was holding a whole world of pain in his heart, that demanded all of his courage. Apple went to the bench and sat next to him.

"The truth can be fantastic ... ever notice how people have all kinds of wonderful dreams sitting on park benches?"

"I never thought of it. ... Today's my birthday," Bill said, melancholic. "Do you like birthdays?"

"What are they for?"

"It's a celebration of the day you were born."

"A great idea! How do you celebrate?"

"With a cake. You put candles on it, then you stand around it and sing a song with your friends. At the end of the song, you make a wish, blow out the candles, and everyone gets a piece of cake."

"How does the song go?"

Bill took a moment to gather his courage. He smiled at the stranger, feeling silly indeed. Only seconds ago, he was convinced this young man had a supernatural quality—yet now he was about to teach him "Happy Birthday." The tenderness of the moment felt so human.

"Wait!" Apple exclaimed. "Perhaps we should dream of a cake and a candle?"

Life has a strange way of unfolding, Bill had always thought; this rendezvous was more than chance. Perhaps the stranger had no message to tell him—maybe he was the message itself.

"Why not?" Bill said, and started singing. "Happy Birthday to you! Happy Birthday to you! Happy Birthday dear ..."

"Bi-ill ..." Apple added.

"... Happy Birthday to you!" the doctor sang, finishing the tune. "You're supposed to cheer afterward," he explained.

"Yay!" Apple cheered. "But you didn't blow out the candle."

Bill took a big breath and blew out the candle on his make-believe cake.

"Happy Birthday, Bill."

"Thank you," he said, checking his watch. "I better get back in there."

"What does a doctor do?"

"People get hurt. They get sick," the doctor explained. "I try to save their lives."

Apple searched in Bill's eyes, looking for the proverbial spark, but he saw reflected there the world and the stars instead. At that moment, staring into the stars burning in Bill's pupils, Apple's memory returned to the moment he had awakened; old Slim's geographical explanation of where they were came to him as a revelation.

"This apple orchard here is in a county, inside a state, inside a country, inside a continent, inside a planet, inside a solar system, inside a galaxy, inside the universe. That was as far as old Slim could see, but he was missing the final container.

"We are dwelling in the infinite mind of the Dreamer!" Apple exclaimed in joy. "The Great Feeling flows through you and me and everything else because we are all creations; there is no place where the Dreamer is not."

Bill looked stunned. Who—or what—was this being who could barely contain the light bursting from his pores? And what was he smiling about?

"I thought I came here seeking my name, but now I see I was brought here for another reason."

"What reason is that?" Bill half wanted to know.

"Human beings think they have a choice, but it is only the way of the dream—the same way that thoughts in our minds always change," said Apple, following the river of dreams. "Nothing is lasting but change; the Dreamer is the source—but unlike the universe that contains, this source is unchangeable."

"Nothing stands still because everything is born, grows, and dies," Bill added. "It is a law of nature."

"Even you and me," Apple agreed, caught up in the breakthrough discovery.

Bill walked a few steps across the garden to a patch of tulips gleaming with dew. The flowers were no less than astonishing, and for an instant, he lost himself in their hues. He could smell the moist earth in the air and the perfume of dozens of flowers. For the first time in years, he listened to birds announce the day and leaves brush one another in the wind. He even noticed a ladybug crawl across a petal and a column of ants march up a trunk; life was everywhere. Bill could not recall a more delightful dawn. Then the name David rang a bell: it was scrawled on a sheet of paper in a file still in the ER. He had initialed it only minutes ago. Could it be possible? Bill's senses were tingling as never before; his suspicions turned into certainty.

"You may think I'm crazy, but I think I know who you are," he whispered, "but I am afraid to tell you ..."

"Don't be afraid, Bill. Dream well," said Apple.

Bill's eyes widened in shock; the true nature of their encounter was revealed.

"You were the voice in my dream!" he gasped, struggling for words. The light of the early sun shimmered through the trees.

I am alive, Apple thought as he looked into the heights, I am awake in the dream. At once he noticed his hand had acquired a glow that spread throughout his being. In bliss he witnessed the rising light embrace the world around him. Apple now felt unsure of how long all these events had taken place—it felt as if light had always been there and that he had been always part of it. The universe was unveiled, erasing all sense of time and space; here was only light and a feeling of love that infused and encompassed everything.

Embraced by luminosity, Apple heard every name and glimpsed every dream in the world; and with a glance, he grasped all that had happened since awakening under the tree.

"We all have a love for life; but life—like death—is a dream. Only love is the truth," Apple said to Bill. "Our dream is an awakening. We are vessels, filled with the Dreamer!" Apple beamed. *The Dream lives through the Dreamer; the Dreamer lives through the Dream.* "The real you is timeless, beyond birth or death."

In that moment, that stretched into eternity, Apple understood who he was and what he did; and so he no longer needed a name. This was his final destination.

"Purpose!" he thought, "the dream has a purpose,.." It all became clear.

"Return to the tree and you will forget who you are not," he said to Bill; his smile forever etched the feeling of joy into the doctor's memory. "You too shall fill your purpose."

"My purpose? I don't know who I am anymore," Bill said to Apple, looking for guidance. "I fear I lost faith in humanity. Like there is no one worth saving."

"There is nothing to fear, for there is nothing outside the Dreamer," Apple offered. "You are well loved. But you must have courage… and faith." Peeking into Bill's eyes, he gazed at the spark he always longed to see: the doctor's dream was luminous, shining among stars, as a light connecting many worlds; it was his gift, his dream. From that moment on, Bill would no longer witness it with the eyes of a stranger.

Dream well. Bill had been waiting for the meaning of those words ever since that day when they'd become his last dream.

"Are you a dream?" The doctor finally asked the stranger.

Yes, I am a dream. That is what I am." Apple responded. "Dream well, Bill." The doctor opened his eyes to admire the tulips as though he had never seen them before.

"Where do I find the tree?" he said, turning to Apple, but no one was there.

Bill was dumbfounded. This was a most wondrous moment. Then something even more extraordinary happened. As he faced the empty bench in shock, the lives he'd saved and comforted came back to him in a tidal wave—gratitude that was met with tears of joy.

"Happy Birthday to you!" singing voices burst in, "Happy Birthday to you! Happy Birthday dear Bi-ill! Happy Birthday to you!"

The entire night staff appeared, carrying a birthday cake filled with lots of candles.

"You thought we forgot?" said one of the nurses, placing the cake on the bench. "Happy birthday, Doctor!"

"That is too many candles," he joked, teary eyed.

"Are you all right?" the nurse asked.

"Yeah," he said. "I just had a dream."

XV
Sweet Dreams

Bill arrived home exhausted that morning, but as he laid in bed, the memory of his encounter with Apple electrified every part of him. Unable to stay still, he leaped from his bed and opened the curtains to let the sunshine in.

"So where is this tree?" he asked the light.

Before he knew it, he was heading in his sports car to the beach. Two hours later he was lost, searching for a field and an apple tree on a lonely road somewhere near the ocean.

Eden Orchards. Bill punched the words into his guidance satellite system; there appeared to be no such place. Then he glimpsed the claw of a giant blue crab beckon from a billboard in the distance. The sign had seen better days, but its faded message could still be read in big bold letters: LE BLUE CRAB RESTAURANT.

As he passed the sign, Bill noticed a patrol car parked behind it. He decided to ask for directions. The young policeman was well used to tourists off the beaten path and recognized the lost city slicker. He carefully got out of his vehicle and stood behind the door with a hand near his holster. Bill backed up his car, and rolling down his passenger window, he flashed an innocent smile.

"Good afternoon officer," he said. "Can you help me? I'm looking for Eden Orchards."

"Eden Orchards?" said the young cop. "Never heard of it."

"Is there a marsh around here? With blue crabs in it?"

"You're a little late for that. The season ended three weeks ago, but the restaurant's open year round." He pointed at the billboard. "It's pretty good."

"Thanks for the tip. Where is the marsh?"

"Head straight ahead into town, take the beach road and follow it through. The marsh will be to your left in about four miles.

"Thank you officer—" Bill said, reading the name on the badge, "—O'Reilly? Do you know a Theresa?"

Officer O'Reilly seemed surprised. He'd never seen this man before, yet the stranger knew something about his family.

"That's my daughter's name. She's nine ... What's your name, sir?"

"Bill Hajid. I'm a doctor."

"And how do you know about my daughter?"

"I don't. I was referring to someone else. This Theresa O'Reilly is older. Quite a coincidence, isn't it?"

"I'll say!" exclaimed the officer, watching the stranger carefully.

"What about apple trees? Any around here?"

"I don't know, sir." The patrolman laughed. "Is there anything else I can help you with?"

"Thanks again, you've been very helpful."

"What are you heading up there for anyways, fishing?"

"No! No, looking for real estate. Are you sure Eden Orchards doesn't ring a bell?"

"As I said, I never heard of it."

Bill smiled, but his thought was in the future. Somehow he knew that Theresa would be a great cop one day.

The town looked like every other along the coast, overcrowded with fast food, souvenir shops, and overpriced seafood dives. Le Blue Crab Restaurant sat like a dinosaur amid neon signs and corporate logos along the strip. Bill pulled over as soon as he saw it. Perhaps he could find an old timer inside who knew the area better.

As Bill was parking his car, the structure next door attracted his attention. The building was in disrepair and looked like a run-down gas station, but the pumps were no longer there; in their place was a sign shaped like a guitar. The afternoon glare on the guitar shop's windows made it hard to see inside, so Bill approached the decrepit building and peered through the dusty glass. The shop had long ago gone out of business. Inside, where instruments once hung against the walls, were their ghosts imprinted on the paint.

"The place is not for sale," came a voice from behind. "After renovations, this will be a café for Le Blue Crab."

Bill turned to see a black man in his sixties, dressed in a business shirt and red tie. He had a soft air about him, as though he walked in exceptionally comfortable shoes.

"This used to be a gas station," Bill remarked.

"Not since I was a little kid," the man told him. "This is old Will's place, bless his soul. He was the pastor of our local church; the man had a beautiful voice! He passed away over ten years ago. His daughter ran the store all these years, but I finally bought it from her—at a fair price, of course!"

"What happened to the garage?" Bill asked. He looked up at the guitar sign.

"Yeah, this here was his father's station, but I guess the ol' boy fancied music more'n anything else, so he turned the place into a guitar shop one day. Everybody thought he was crazy, but he stayed opened for thirty years! Would you like to have a nice crab stew? Best in the county!"

"Do you to know where Eden Orchards is?"

"Eden Orchards? Sweet Lord! Haven't heard that name in a long time! That's what the apple field used to be called, before they built warehouses on it. My momma used to tell me about it. Kids would get free apples by the bucket. You know, now that I think of it, I swear right behind the warehouses between the roads, there is still a quarter mile patch of it"

"How do I get there?" asked Bill.

"It's on the other side of the marsh. Just go straight down the road and you'll find it. Can't miss it… You sure you don't want some crab stew?"

Bill thanked the man and got into his car, ready to drive down to the shore; but as he was pulling out of the parking lot, he noticed a lonely bench overlooking the ocean at the edge of the dunes. He turned onto the road, smiling to himself at the images the bench evoked, when he almost ran over a blind man crossing the street with his dog. The duo stopped short as soon as the dog heard squealing brakes.

"I'm very sorry!" Bill shouted from his seat—he had missed them by a scant few feet. The blind man turned to face him and, without saying a word, appeared to look straight at him. He then crossed the street with his dog and headed straight toward the water.

This route was full of clues, and although Bill could not decipher them, they passed like birds overhead.

A three o'clock sun etched the landscape and made it glow. Bill drove along the marsh road, enchanted by its beauty, when he spotted gray warehouses in the distance. Deep in thought, Bill failed to notice a park ranger pulling out from a small dirt road. Both vehicles slammed on their brakes and came to a screeching stop. The ranger in the vehicle waved him to move ahead.

THEO ANDROPULOS NATURAL MARSH LIFE PRESERVATION PARK read the sign on the ranger's door.

Theo, Bill rejoiced in anticipation. He was close to his destination. The signs were all in place.

"Who is Theo Andropulos?" Bill politely asked the driver.

"Mister Andropulos was our founder, he used to own the marshlands," the park ranger answered curtly. "If you would like to know more about the park, come back during the weekend, there is a small museum open at the end of the marsh next to the storage warehouses."

"Thank you," said Bill, "much obliged," and he continued down the beach road. Within minutes he arrived at the edge of the marsh, along a plain that extended toward the warehouses. He pulled into the parking lot of the tiny park museum and headed straight to the fence that surrounded the complex.

"How I am supposed to forget who I am not?" he asked, confused, as he stared at the industrial buildings before him. Under any other circumstance, Bill would have considered his actions madness, but something was telling him otherwise—and this time, Bill was determined to do the right thing.

"Dream well," he repeated.

He walked along the fence until he reached the top of a knoll. From here he could see a cluster of warehouses extending to a valley that rolled into the sea. Closing his eyes, Bill imagined what this all must have looked like once. How beautiful! he thought. All those apples growing on trees in a tall field, above the water!

"It must have been breathtaking," he said aloud and opened his eyes to the ugly reality that lay before him; but to his surprise, he saw a pretty patch of land away in the distance—a small hidden valley beyond the industrial park. Bill rushed along the edge of the property trying to find a way in, until at last he reached the bottom of the rise, and invigorated, he charged up the hill.

By the time Bill reached the top of the hill, what he beheld filled him with bliss. Here it was, right out of his dream: a single apple tree grown wild, a few hundred yards from what once had been an orchard. Majestic and solitary, it towered in the midst of a field, as though a single fruit had fallen far from the tree and flowered on its own. Bill looked at it, transfixed. The apple tree gently waved its branches and the sweet scent of blossoms perfumed the air. He half expected a ghost to appear or to hear Apple's words in the wind; instead, he had only a feeling.

"Mmmm, oohh …"

Bill noticed a sound coming from the tree, one he had heard before and knew well: the faint cry of a person moaning in pain, and it sounded very real.

"Slim?" he whispered, hesitant.

"Hey kid," Slim rasped, "you're back!"

Bill checked the old man's pulse; it was a miracle he was alive. He had been lying all night on the cold damp ground, hidden in the grass. Half conscious and dazed from the pain of broken bones and a nasty blow to the head, old Slim survived the fall by refusing to relinquish his only possession, a mighty love for life; he was not yet ready to let go.

"What did you think of the world?" The old man smiled. "Isn't it something!"

"We've got to get you to a hospital," Bill told him.

"What are you calling yourself these days, kid?"

"Bill," he said, "I'm a doctor."

"I think I felt off the tree, Bill," said Slim, "I thought you were a dream."

"I am," responded the doctor, feeling a tingle in his heart, a caress. Just as Apple had predicted, he no longer remembered who he was not; his quest had ended and a journey of the spirit had begun.

A wind from the south carried the scent of apple blossoms out of the valley, into the warehouses and past the marsh below. The crabs would return next year to repeat their exodus to the sea, the tree would renew its fruits, and in that fraction of time, a million human dreams would sprout like wildflowers across the world, a glorious reminder of the love that created them.

"Dream well," he heard in his mind. Bill rejoiced.

Change is the way of the dream: the living mind changes as the seasons, fluttering like butterfly wings, as real as the tree, as fantastic as infinity, as simple to behold as the view from a lone park bench.

As for Apple, he remains inside our dream. To those who met him he was nothing short of a miracle but for all the reasons that matter we can rest assured of one thing, he is you and me, and everybody else, miraculously becoming what is most needed just at the right moment, gaining purpose when there is no safety glass. So the next time you come across a stranger that mysteriously appears just when you need it, pay attention for the apple never falls far from the tree; it is nothing less than the human spirit, ever willing to make a dream come true.

About the author:

Luis Aira was born in Cuba and raised in Venezuela. He moved to the United States as a teen and attended Emerson College in Boston. He is a critically acclaimed filmmaker and writer with a long career in the visual arts. He is the author of "Somewhere", a children's novel illustrated by Sergio Arau. Mr. Aira lives in Los Angeles.

For more info go to: www.luisaira.com

"The Dreamer"
by Luis Aira
Cover Art by Edward Walton Wilcox
Luis Aira Copyright © 2010
Registered ® WGA
ISBN# 978-0-578-05347-9